Corn Dolls

Foxton Girls

We All Fall Down

The House of Secrets

CORN DOLLS

AN O'MALLEY & SWIFT NOVEL

K.T. GALLOWAY

For my daughter. My world.

BLURB

Some Games Can Kill You.

A young girl is missing. Snatched from her home during a game of hide and seek. Left behind in her place is a doll crudely twisted from stalks of corn.

Psychotherapist Annie O'Malley thought she'd left the police force forever. The trouble is she thinks she knows the identity of the killer, and she's the only one who can hunt him down before it's too late.

O'Malley is drawn back to a world she thought she'd escaped, to a case where every turn reminds her of her childhood and her missing sister. When she's partnered with DI Joe Swift, a man with more ghosts than people in his past, O'Malley has to make the hardest decision of her life.

Save a stranger. Or save herself.

ONE

Sunday

"… NINETY-EIGHT, NIGHTY-NINE, ONE HUNDRED. HERE I come, ready or not."

Maggie Finch opened her eyes expecting to see her daughter half-hiding behind the curtains. At four years old it was always the curtains, or under the covers of the beds, occasionally in the pantry—but that was only when there were biscuits on offer, and the last few weeks had been quite tight for money, so the biscuit tin was empty.

"Orla?" Maggie sing-songed, as she started searching in earnest.

She hauled her weary body off the sagging couch and stretched to the ceiling.

It's easier when it's the curtains.

"Orla?" she sang again, peeking behind the curtains just in case.

There was no-one there. Just an obstructed view out to the North Norfolk salt marshes beyond the old Ford Ka standing rusty in the drive, and the knee-high weeds in the front garden. Another chore to add to the ever-increasing list.

Maggie sighed and went to check behind the rest of the downstairs curtains.

Please be downstairs. Please be downstairs.

But the curtains gave up no answers. The thought of hauling her body up the narrow stairs when she couldn't even see down to her feet anymore made Maggie want to throw herself back on the sofa and fall asleep. She was sure she hadn't been this exhausted last time around. When she had been pregnant with Orla, she had been the epitome of blooming. Now she was just fat and tired. But she hadn't been doing it all on her own back then, with a four-year-old to deal with on top of it all.

He's such a dick.

Maggie pulled back the heavy curtains that were drawn over the front door to keep out the draught. Not that there should be draughts in August, but these old flint houses held the cold as if it had burrowed into their bones, and every little bit of warmth was precious.

"Gotcha!" she yelled, laughing.

But there was no-one there either. Maggie rattled the handle.

Still locked.

She turned around. The stairs loomed over her like Everest. They may as well have been an unattainable mountain peak the way she was feeling. But when her daughter wanted to play hide and seek, she went along with it, even if it was just for the hundred seconds of peace while she was counting.

The bannister was barely attached to the wall, the lime plaster around the fixings giving up the ghost before Maggie had even moved in. But there was no other way of

2

getting up there safely. She took a deep breath and placed her foot on the first step.

"I'm coming to get you," she growled, hoping that Orla's squeals would give away her position.

She also hoped that Orla wouldn't want her to take a turn at hiding next. Really, as an adult there were few places to hide effectively anyway. At eight months pregnant those places were almost non-existent.

The upper floor of the old flint cottage was smaller than downstairs. Maggie often thought about this weird curveball of physics, given that the house looked symmetrical from each axis. But today she was thankful for the anomaly. Only two bedrooms and a creaky old airing cupboard to check. And Orla had been known to run as fast as she could past the airing cupboard to get from the stairs to her bedroom at the back of the house. There was always a witch or a ghost or a baddie lurking behind the door. The noise of the water tank could quite easily be a dragon or a howling wind, bringing with it some unseen threat that would exponentially develop in Orla's mind until she was screaming with hysterical terror, until she reached the safety of her bed.

Maggie's own room was at the top of the stairs, so she checked there first. The mattress on her bed looked inviting, despite sagging almost to the floor. But a small cold niggle of fear was starting to spread its fingers through Maggie's stomach. The house was quiet. Too quiet. Orla was never normally not emitting some sort of noise, even when she was asleep. Was she stepping her hiding game up a notch?

Yes, that's probably it. She's very competitive when it comes to hiding.

Maggie shook out her own curtains, revealing

nothing but a cloud of dust. Coughing, she undid the latch and pushed open her window, breathing in the fresh, salty air, feeling it stick to her face the way it clung to everything it touched. Maggie's window looked out over the marshes and onto the North Sea. Even today, with the sun belting through the mist brought in by the water, the sea looked cold and dirty. The tide was out, leaving behind a liminal landscape of twisted, muddy creeks dotted with purple specks of sea lavender. It should be beautiful, but Maggie had always found it left her with an ominous sense of unease; the Pied Piper luring the children to their watery fate with his hypnotic tunes.

There was something amiss. Maggie couldn't quite put her finger on it. Was it the way the water was throwing itself about in waves with no direction; tops white with froth, hiding the treacherous sandbanks underneath? Was it the lonely piping of the oystercatchers?

Maggie tried to calm her breathing, wrapping her arms around her bump. She must protect her unborn child.

I can't even look after the one I have. What hope is there?

"Orla!" Maggie shouted now, the fun sapped from her voice.

There was no way Orla could be under Maggie's bed, it was too low. And there was nowhere else she could have hidden in Maggie's small room. The walls closed in on Maggie as she half ran out of the room and threw open the airing cupboard door. The water tank grumbled as she threw towels onto the landing floor, but they gave up nothing but empty shelves.

"Orla, answer Mummy now. Let's have a snack. How about some chocolate?" Maggie lied. There was no choco-

4

late, but a screaming, angry Orla was better than no Orla at all.

The rush of blood in Maggie's ears sounded just like the sea. Orla knew not to go anywhere near the sea, didn't she? Maggie had drummed it into her since she was born. Besides, the front door was still locked.

"ORLA!"

Something wasn't right. Ducking into Orla's room, Maggie gave it a cursory check. The bed was still neatly made. The curtains threadbare and practically see-through. She wasn't there. There were no other places in the tiny space that could hide even a four-year-old.

Maggie stumbled over her own feet as she tried to turn in the doorway. The narrow landing seemed to lengthen as she ran towards the stairs. The rail shook under her weight as she descended, rattling loud enough to be heard over her shouts for her daughter. The bottom step, worn into a curve with use over a hundred years, came up to meet Maggie quicker than she expected, her foot slipped out from under her and she landed with a crunch on her coccyx, the wind completely knocked out of her lungs. *Everywhere* hurt, her bump felt too heavy to lift back up again, but she had no choice other than to get back up and find Orla.

There was no one else to help. Maggie spoke in whispers to her parents every day, she missed them so much. But the truth was, they had both left her a long time ago. Orla's dad had skipped out a month ago, two years after moving them all out to the arse end of nowhere because it was more convenient for his work, never mind the fact his wife and daughter were now alone for days at a time. Neither of them had heard a word from him since the day he left.

Maybe he's come back.

Maggie would have laughed at the idea was it not for the sheer paralysing terror coursing through her body. She wanted to call someone, have someone tell her everything would be okay. Most probably, Orla was so proud of her new hiding place that she didn't want to give it up, not even for chocolate. A sob bubbled up in Maggie's throat.

"Orla!" she cried. "Where are you?"

Her bump had felt lower over the last few days, her new baby was getting ready to meet the world. Not long now, Maggie could tell. She gathered it up in her arms as best she could and limped through the living room to the kitchen. She would check the downstairs again. Maybe Orla was creeping silently between hiding places, making the game more fun.

The house was still. How many times could Maggie check each room before she gave in to the idea that Orla wasn't here? She needed to talk it through with someone else, allay her fears with a friendly voice, because calling the police felt too extreme. It was just a game of hide and seek. They'd laugh at her for being over-dramatic. But there was no one else to talk to. Apart from the old couple next door, who already thought Maggie was a bad mother, her only neighbours were the sea birds.

The clock in the kitchen ticked despite the layer of fat clogging the gears, counting down the minutes Orla had been missing. What else could Maggie do? It was almost supper time. Orla was ruled by her internal food clock. Maybe Maggie could sit it out and wait for her daughter to get hungry. She walked over to the door and checked it was still locked.

Did I check this one last time?

Maggie was sure she hadn't. So when it swung open,

the pit of dread in her stomach dropped lower, like icy liquid sloshing around in her bowels.

"ORLA," Maggie shouted into the weeds at the back.

Still in her bare feet, Maggie stepped out onto the gravel. The garden was small, like the rest of the cottage. A little square of cowslips and dandelions. Maggie crunched around the side of the cottage to the front—and the open gate.

Please, no.

Shaking with fear, Maggie shuffled down the path, past the old car and out onto the stretch of tarmac. She looked left and right, hoping to spot the bright blonde hair flashing in the sun. Nothing. Behind the tarmac was the salt marsh, dipping away from the road with clusters of reeds that looked soft and friendly, hiding the deep mud below.

"ORLA!"

She didn't want to look. If she didn't look, everything would be okay.

The tarmac was hot on Maggie's bare soles as she walked to the edge of the road. Leaning as far forwards as was safe with her shift in balance, she peered into the reeds. There was nothing there but thick black mud. Another sob escaped. Tears ran down Maggie's cheeks and she wiped them away with the cuff of her sleeve.

"Orla, please!" she cried, turning back to face the cottage.

Something caught her eye at the front door. She squinted in the sun, her hand up to shadow her view.

What the…?

Stumbling back across the road, Maggie felt the bile rising up into her throat. She didn't notice the sharp stones of the driveway under her feet, or the stinging nettles grabbing at her ankles as she shuffled along the path. A pair of starlings nesting in the roof swooped down at her, so close that the wind from their wings whipped at her face. The rooks chattered in the trees, clacking loudly a warning for all to hear. Maggie's head spun.

The tears streaming from Maggie's eyes distorted the front door until its shape was a surrealist Dali image. The paint—long since stripped back with the strength of the salt in the air—was such a dull blue that even with her less than perfect vision the object nailed to the wood stood out like an angry blight. Maggie reached a shaking hand up, afraid to touch it but unable to stop. Wiping her eyes dry with the back of her other hand, Maggie could see it wasn't a clump of straw at all, but a crudely twisted corn husk, tied into the faceless shape of a woman.

A corn doll.

"ORLA!" Maggie screamed as the all-consuming fear and horror sent her sobbing to her knees.

TWO

Monday

"So, can I go now?"

Annie held in a sigh, trying to remain professional when all she really wanted to do was scream, *You've only been here for five minutes and all you've done is tell me how unfair it is that you can't go and score gear anymore!*

"Maybe let's try setting some goals before you leave?" she said instead. "Then we can look back next week and see how far you've come."

"What? I have to come *back*?" The man looked perplexed. He picked at the skin around his thumbnail as his legs jittered up and down in the comfortable chair.

Annie was used to it. Hardly anyone who came to see her wanted to come back again. She would probably take it personally if they weren't sent directly from the probation service as part of the conditions of their bail.

"How about we start with what you missed the most

while you were inside? The things you felt you couldn't do without. Maybe those can be your priority now you *are* out? Any family or friends? A sport to start or a new hobby to take up? Or something for your wellbeing; a haircut to plan, or a meal to prepare. It can be anything that you would find positive and easy to engage in," Annie prompted, handing the young man a new notebook and a Bic biro from her stash.

His cuticles were red raw, and his hands shook as he took hold of the stationery, eyeing it warily as though Annie had just offered him napalm. His grey tracksuit looked standard issue and Annie couldn't help but notice old track marks on his arms when he had rolled up his sleeves. Nothing phased her anymore; after almost ten years working with probationers Annie had seen it all, and she was still only thirty-five.

The young man exclaimed; his eyes lit up with an idea.

"Well, there was this new skunk on the street just as I was lifted. I'd like to try some of that. I kept thinking about it when I was locked up. It sounded wicked, man." He wiped his nose on the back of his hand and opened the notebook.

Oh, dear God. She may have seen it all, and heard even more, but that didn't make it easier when she was working against the tide.

"How about we start with something legal?" she said, trying to keep the smile plastered on her face. "Something that won't lead to you being recalled back to prison for breaking the conditions of your parole."

He started chewing the end of the pen, slurping it loudly. When he didn't come up for air, Annie side-eyed the clock. It was coming up to the end of his thirty minutes, but she wasn't going to stretch out this session to make up for his lack of engagement. He was still mulling over what was important to him that he couldn't inject, smoke, or inhale, so Annie let her eyes wander, giving him the space to come up with some realistic goals.

Outside, the sky looked heavy, like a wet dishcloth needing to be wrung out. There would be thunder later, Annie was sure of it. The day had been too hot, too close, the pressure had felt thick around her skull since she'd rolled out of bed and started working. She shook the tension from her jaw and turned her attention back to the young probationer.

"So, what do you think?"

He shook his head at her.

"Nope, I can't think of anything. Can I go now?" he asked, bouncing to his feet and heading to the door.

His time was almost up and Annie knew when she was fighting a losing battle. She stood up and held out her hand.

"Homework then," she said, as he bounced back to her and shook her offered hand, his fingers cold and damp. "Try and think of at least a couple of small goals you'd like to achieve while we're working together. Probation states it will be at least twelve weeks, so we have plenty of time."

Annie walked towards the door of her small office and held it open for her newest client, shaking her head as he tried to hand back the soaking pen.

"You keep it, you can use it to write up your homework."

The young man looked chuffed.

"Thanks Miss O'Malley. See you around."

Annie shut the door behind him and leant her body

against it, fighting the urge to slump to the floor. She was exhausted.

The idea of being a private sector psychotherapist had been firmly fixed in her sights throughout her two years of postgraduate training. Annie had pictured herself in an academic office with shelves of books lining the walls; working with clients to achieve goals to make their lives more meaningful. A makeshift office above a pizza parlour on an old cobbled street in Norwich, taking parole clients from the inadequately paying government wasn't quite that picture. Still, it was a good job and Annie enjoyed the variety of people who came through her door each day. They weren't all young men troubled by illicit substances that Annie may or may not have sampled herself during her undergraduate university days, which already were a good fifteen years behind her.

"Dinner?" Annie asked the pot plant sitting on the windowsill.

The plant remained stoic, but she took that as an affirmative. Locking the door to the office behind her, Annie skipped down the stairs and out into the street. The sun was dropping, and the cobbled street shone like amber and steel. The shops were long shut, the bars and cafes were coming into their own with the hustle and bustle of the small city.

Stepping out of the way of a group of drunken young women as they giggled conspiratorially, Annie scoured their faces hurriedly before they could pass her by.

Is it you, Mim? Are you here?

But they passed by without a second glance, and hope escaped from her body like a slow puncture. She sighed and pushed the door to the pizzeria open, the tinkling of the bell above triggering a Pavlovian response.

"Annie!" A man in chef's whites and a dusty apron waved at her from behind the counter. "The usual?"

Annie nodded and waved back. She took up residence in her seat by the window and grabbed her laptop out of her bag. Booting it up, she started to type up her client notes from the last assessment of the day. It had been a busy day, five clients in total. Annie loved her job; the client-centred goal-setting was an important way for her to engage with her probationers, but more often than not they saw her as a chance to have freedom. A means to an end. And ten years in, Annie was finding her tether a lot shorter than when she had started out. Still, anything was better than the six months she'd spent as a police constable straight out of university, carrying an undergraduate degree in Psychology and a naive will to make a difference.

Another gaggle of women passed by the window, leaning into the tinted glass to check their makeup, not knowing Annie was on the other side searching their faces for Mim. Annie caught sight of herself in the reflection as they left. She could have been her younger sister's twin, yet there were fifteen years between them. Her regular English roses and cream complexion had taken on a grey hint these last few months. She pinched her cheeks to try and look less like Morticia Addams, though with her coppery autumn ringlets and bright green eyes, she couldn't be further from the macabre family if she tried. Annie sighed and went back to her notes, feeling them clogging her brain like a mundane chore.

Maybe it *was* time for a change. Was it fair to carry on seeing people when it felt like this? Didn't she owe them more than the bare minimum? Annie snorted a laugh, what else was she going to do? It wasn't like there were lots of options for someone in their mid-thirties with a work history that consisted of ten years in the same job and a failed police career.

The smell of pizza drew Annie out of her reverie.

"Here you go, one deep pan veggie delight, with added mushrooms," the man in the chef's whites said, placing her dinner in front of her with a flourish. "And a large glass of Malbec."

"You're a star, Pete," Annie said, her mouth watering in anticipation. "Thanks."

The chef smiled and turned to walk away.

"Oh, Pete." Annie stopped him. "I'll not be in for dinner tomorrow, I've got a networking event with the prison service."

She shuddered comically at Pete's grimace.

"I'll see you Wednesday then, and you can tell me all about it," he winked, and left Annie to her pizza.

Networking was the least favourite part of Annie's job and she wondered now, as she devoured the pizza, if this was what was causing her work slump. Twice yearly, the prison service held a get-together for its extended work family, and twice yearly, Annie felt like a prune as she shook hands with consultants and psychiatrists who still looked down on what she did.

Draining her glass, she dropped a fiver on the table as a tip and gathered herself for home. She stepped out of the pizzeria, shouting her thanks to Pete.

Unlocking the door to the stairwell, Annie headed back up to the office, her heart as heavy as her feet. She pulled down the blinds, blocking out the light from the street-lamps and casting the small room into darkness. Feeling her way through to the kitchenette, Annie switched on the small kettle, then thought better of it and pulled the stopper out of a bottle of red she had stashed in an overhead cupboard. Pouring what was left into a tumbler, she went back through to the office space and pulled out a camp bed and sleeping bag from under the sofa. Grunting as she opened it out, Annie made her bed for the night.

Nope, definitely not how I was imagining my life.

Her laptop pinged with an email and Annie grabbed it from her bag and took it over to the camp bed. The springs gave an unholy screech as she made herself comfortable, the bed having seen better days during Annie's teen years when her numerous friends would pile on to it during sleepovers. When she'd asked her mum for a loan of the old bed, she'd hoped this would be the last thing her mother would picture Annie using it for.

Hitting the touchpad over the mail icon, Annie's heart rate smashed through the thatched roof above when she saw the cost of this month's invoice. She spent a large proportion of her time teaching others how to recognise when people were taking advantage of them, schooling them on their budgeting and life skills, yet here she was paying inordinate amounts of money—plus her whole life savings—to a private investigator who came up empty-handed every month. But as quickly as her anger rose up, so did her frail hope.

It might happen next time. The next lead might be the one. I can't give up on Mim now.

She'd deal with that in the morning; for now, all she had the energy left to do was watch a rerun of *Spooks* and drink her tumbler of wine. Closing her laptop lid, a story in the news bar caught Annie's eye. A flicker of recognition ran through her at the familiar face dominating the head-line. She snapped the laptop back open and clicked on the link: recognition soon giving way to a cold trickle of fear.

Police are on the hunt for the father of a missing child.

The young girl went missing from her family home some-time yesterday evening. Police believe that she may have been abducted and are appealing for those who were in the area to get in contact with them. They are also very keen to get in contact with the child's father. Anyone with informa-tion to call local police on...

Ignoring the sensationalised writing of the red top press, Annie scanned the screen, jotting down the contact number on her phone, freezing at the forlorn picture of a heavily pregnant woman and the indented addition of the missing girl. The photograph of the father in question, the photo that had caught her attention, was a skinny-faced man with eyes sunken from the effects of years of drug abuse. Tim Barclay, a man she had been working with up until four weeks ago when he'd been a no-show, and she hadn't seen or heard from him since.

THREE

Tuesday

It was a Tuesday morning. Yet the whole of the city seemed to be congregating around the entrance to the police station.

"Excuse me," Annie said, breathing in to squeeze between two very vocal women with large placards that were threatening to take her eye out.

They glared at her as she pulled open the glass doors and fell through into the reception. It was quiet in here. The gentle tap of a keyboard and the smell of coffee rose to greet her like an old friend. Though it was only once a month that Annie set foot in the city headquarters for work —the main police building having been relocated to the outskirts of the ever-increasing city over ten years ago now —she always felt comforted that nothing much had changed here.

The receptionist glanced over, double-taking at Annie, and smiled.

"Annie, thank goodness," she said, waving her hand to call Annie over. "I thought maybe the mobs had broken the invisible barricade and stormed the building. How are you?"

Annie smiled.

"Oh, you know, Rose," she said, not really wanting to go into how she was sleeping in her office, hating her job, and generally feeling pretty crap about life to the poor woman, who always seemed so upbeat. "What's with the crowds?"

Rose rolled her eyes. "They're protesting. They've been here for the last couple of days. Thing is, they're not very organised, they just turn up at eight, stand at the door, then go home again at tea time, every single bloody day!"

"What are they protesting?" Annie asked, turning back to look at the crowd milling by the entrance.

"Don't make eye contact with them," Rose hissed lightly. "They'll try to accost you on the way out, then you'll be stuck there until teatime too."

They both laughed.

"They're protesting the cuts," Rose continued. "The cuts to the services that the government deem non-essential. You know, the allied health, advocates, mental health workers, day services."

Annie screwed up her face. "Maybe I *should* go and join them." She shrugged.

"We all disagree with the cuts, but they're protesting in the wrong place. They need County Hall, or Ten Downing Street, not their local cop shop." Rose shook her head. "Anyway, you here for your supervision? Shall I get Marion?"

"God no!" Annie blurted, very much not wanting to see her boss, and Rose burst out laughing. "As much as I'd love to be grilled on my workload and ethic at nine on a Tuesday morning, I'll be seeing Marion tonight at the networking thing, so I'll prolong that joy until then. No, I've got a meeting with DI Joe Swift."

Rose raised an eyebrow. "I'll let him know you're here. Take a seat, love. And I'll see you tonight if I don't see you before. Yay." Her enthusiasm for the event mirrored Annie's.

Annie took a seat under a poster board advertising neighbourhood watch and translation services dotted between lost cats and bikes for sale. The station was a weird mix of old and new. Blue plastic seats, flooring that felt tacky underfoot, yet the doors leading to the inner sanctum were shiny glass and electric and opened only at the scan of a pass card. Annie studied her nails as she waited for DI Swift to appear. She was nervous. Normally she would meet with Marion in her office, discuss concerns about clients, possible new referrals, then head off into the city for a proper coffee to take the taste of police station coffee out of her mouth. This time she was here to meet with *actual* police and not just a paper-wielding civil servant whose sole purpose in life was to make people miserable.

"Ms O'Malley?"

DI Swift was tall, and broad, and very attractive.

"Miss," Annie replied, standing and offering her hand. "But please, call me Annie."

She heard Rose stifle a snort from behind her desk.

"DI Swift," he replied, smiling knowingly. "Please follow me."

Annie waited until DI Swift had turned away, then she shot Rose a look.

Oh my god, she mouthed to her old friend, who started making a lewd gesture behind the DI's back.

Annie followed DI Swift through the fancy new doors and into the corridors behind. The coffee smell grew stronger and the noise of keyboards, printers, and chatter grew louder.

"Just in here," he held a door open and Annie walked past him into what must have been an interview room.

"Ooh," she gasped, her nerves making her brain feel like porridge. "I hope I'm not in any trouble."

She nodded at the tape recorder and the one-way glass, which were giving off a heady scent of stereotype.

"Please take a seat," DI Swift laughed politely at her joke and now Annie felt like she really *was* in trouble. "Can I get you a drink? Tea, coffee, water?"

"I've tasted the coffee here. So no, thanks. I had one before I came out." Annie shook her head.

"Wise move," DI Swift laughed properly this time. He sat down at the table opposite Annie, rolling his shirt sleeves up as though he was about to set himself to task. "We appreciate the call, Miss O'Malley. So, what can you tell me about Orla Finch's father?"

Annie thought for a moment. It had been just over a month since her last session with Tim Barclay. She was sure the police would already know everything she was about to say, and felt, all of a sudden, childish for having made the call.

"Look, I'm sure there's not a lot I can tell you that you don't already know," she said, staring at the blank mirror behind DI Swift's head, hoping the room on the other side was empty. One person hearing her spout useless information was enough to contend with. "I worked with him as a therapist as part of his probation under the MHTR, the Mental Health Treatment Requirement, after he was given a custodial sentence for common assault and ABH. Tim was given 15 months but was out in seven with his conditions. I think he was also under the Drug Rehab Requirement too. I can't go into what we talked about because of confidentiality. But I can say that he didn't turn up to his last appointment with me. Of course, I let Marion know, but I didn't chase him. That's up to the probation officer."

Swift dipped his chin.

"Sorry, Marion Farmer. She's Regional Offender Manager. My boss!"

"Yeah, I know who she is, she's based in our station and rather infamous," he said wryly.

Annie felt herself blush. *Of course he knew Marion, everyone knows Marion.* "Yes, sorry. Um… so that was a little over four weeks ago. He just never showed. And it surprised me, to be honest. He'd seemed keen to atone for what he'd done. Wrong place, wrong time, wrong batch of drugs. I never felt he was just there to tick a box, and I get that a lot."

DI Swift shifted in his seat, leaning forwards towards Annie.

"You're right," he said, propping his head up on his elbows. "We do already know all of that. Is there anything you can tell me that we *don't* know? What he was like as a person. How he felt about his daughter. How he felt about his now-ex. Things like that."

Annie chewed the inside of her cheek. She wasn't sure if telling DI Swift more about Tim Barclay was breaking her client confidentiality pact, but getting a warrant took time, and Annie didn't want to be the reason between the life and death of a four-year-old girl.

"He was a nice guy," she said, eventually. "Like, I'd happily have a conversation with him in the pub. He was funny and intelligent. But when he had been using, I couldn't get a coherent sentence out of him, let alone a story. It was like he was two different people. But that's often the case, isn't it? When someone turns to drugs. And he doted on that little girl, and his partner. I didn't know things had gone wrong between him and Maggie Finch."

"So he did talk about Orla then?" DI Swift asked, sitting up a bit straighter.

Annie nodded warily. "Yes, he did, but not in a way that would indicate he was going to steal her away from her life. More in a remorseful *what have I done* kind of a way. Look, I'm not sure I should be saying more without his consent, but I don't think he would have it in him to harm his own child."

"Even if he was using?"

Annie shrugged. Truth be told, people were capable of anything when they were high. She should know.

"Can I ask you one more thing?" DI Swift said, running his hands through his hair.

"Sure."

"Did you ever get the impression that Tim was into weird stuff?"

Annie almost laughed, but the look on DI Swift's face stopped her.

"Weird stuff?" she asked.

"Yeah, you know, *weird* stuff."

"You're going to have to elaborate. You can't just throw *weird* in off the bat and expect me to have a clue what you're on about."

DI Swift rubbed his face hard enough to leave his skin pink.

"Do you know Maggie Finch, the mum, well?" He was changing tact.

"I met her briefly a couple of times at the very beginning of my work with Tim. But otherwise, not really, why?"

"I think you're going to be useful, I need all the help I can get on this. I'm going to bring you in," DI Swift said, as though he had already asked Annie and got her permission.

"What?" Annie was overwhelmed at the very idea she could be *just brought in* on a case, let alone thinking about her clients and the backlog of paperwork she was already sitting on, and that's not even mentioning her failed police career. But she couldn't deny the little flame of excitement that had just ignited in her. "Are you allowed to do that?"

DI Swift looked Annie right in the eyes.

"I'm SIO on this case, pretty sure I can bring in a consultant," he said, pulling his chin up before dropping it again quickly and pleading instead. "Look, being totally transparent, I did a background check on you and I know you were in the force previously, plus you're already working for the probation service and you're DBS checked. You'd be doing me a favour, Miss O'Malley, Annie. There are things about this case that are unsettling. Maggie Finch has clammed up, I need your help in bringing her out again. You can get people to talk, can't you?"

"I'm not the CIA!"

DI Swift laughed, dropping the tension in the room by a few notches.

"I was thinking more AC12, as long as I can be Hastings."

"Does that mean I'm Steve Arnott?"

"You can be H as far as I'm concerned, as long as you can get Orla's mum to talk. We're over twenty-four hours into a child abduction case and we have no leads, and everything we've tried has been a dead end."

Annie felt the temperature drop by a couple of degrees with the DI's words.

"Okay Detective Inspector Swift, I'll help as best I can. But you'll need to agree it with my boss."

"Consider it done." DI Swift stood up from his chair. "I'll see you out. And I'll be in touch as soon as I have confirmation."

They walked out the same way they had come. The crowd of protesters still hung about the front door of the building and Annie heard the detective mutter under his breath at their ill-directed persistence.

"Oh, and Annie," DI Swift said as he opened the front door onto the crowd for her. "It's Swift, or Boss. Drop the DI, and don't ever think about calling me Guv."

Annie smiled to herself as she headed down the steps through the throngs of people. Maybe this case—and Swift —were just what she needed.

FOUR

"O'MALLEY, GET YOUR ARSE OVER HERE NOW AND LET ME kick it to kingdom come!"

Annie shrank a little inside as she stepped into the conference room in a middle rate hotel on the outskirts of the city.

At least let me get my coat off before you say your welcomes!

"Hi Marion," she said, mustering a smile. "Nice to see you too."

At five foot nothing, with a sleek bob that made her look like Edna from *The Incredibles,* Marion had a cold smile that didn't reach her eyes. Annie joined the group of people surrounding the woman, who all looked as though they were being held against their will. Grabbing a glass of champagne from a passing waiter, Annie scoped the other members of the group. She recognised a couple of them from the station, including Rose, who caught her eye and withered surreptitiously at Marion. There was another probation officer, and one of Annie's psychotherapy team who worked over in Cambridgeshire.

The other lucky members, Annie didn't know, but that didn't stop Marion reprimanding her in front of them anyway.

"What's this I hear about you being poached by Joe Swift?" she shouted.

Rose stifled a surprised noise and muttered how she had been waiting much longer to be poached by Swift. Annie felt herself blush as everyone's eyes turned their focus on her.

"It's just for this case he's working now," she said. "It's not forever, and I'm still working as a psychotherapist with my giant caseload too!"

"Yes, well." Marion looked like her head was about to explode, her face puce, her eyes bright. "It would have been nice to have been consulted first, seeing as I'm your boss, young lady. And Swift has demanded you full time, so I'm reallocating your cases."

Annie wanted the ground to open up and swallow her whole. Marion was normally condescending and trite, but it was usually just the two of them. Not a networking event where people came to meet and greet. And now, those who didn't know Annie, had just heard her being talked to like a child. So much for making a good impression.

She bit her tongue. Retaliation wasn't worth risking her job, at least not while she was sleeping on an ancient camp bed in her office, anyway.

"It was all very last minute," she went for instead. "I couldn't say no, there's a child's life at stake."

Try arguing with that one!

Marion made a noise that could either be an agreement or a reprimand and turned her attention back to one of the women Annie didn't know. Rose took the chance to peel herself away and grabbed Annie's arm, guiding her away from the pint-sized boss and towards the back of the room, where the other reprobates were hanging out.

"You never said you were going to be working with Swift?!" she hissed. "God, I'd give my right arm and leg if I could work with him for even one day."

"Shhh," Annie said, turning her head to check no-one was listening in. "It's just for one case, and *only* because I've worked with a member of the family of the missing girl."

"You know his back story, right?" Rose sighed.

"I know some of it, but I can't talk about a client without breaking confidentiality and I certainly can't talk about it here and now."

"No," Rose interrupted. "*Swift's* back story? I don't care about your case. Except the missing girl, obvs. We all want her back safe and sound. No, Swift comes with baggage bigger than T-Swizzle." She giggled, then hiccupped.

Annie suddenly realised just how much Rose must have had to drink already to drown out the sorrows of being cornered by Marion. Annie nodded towards the fire escape, which was propped open for the smokers, and they headed out to the empty courtyard.

"T-Swizzle?" Annie asked, when they had made themselves comfortable at an old wooden picnic bench with an overflowing ashtray.

"Taylor Swift! Ha! Her and Joe could be related," Rose said, her eyes sparkling. "Anyway…Joe. His wife took off last year. Apparently, she went out for a walk and then… poof, vanished into thin air. No one knows if it was intentional or not, but it was a bit odd in the office for a time; apparently there's no active case for her. He went off the rails a bit, understandably, and this is his first case back.

All I'm saying is, he's got issues. Oh and he's probably still married."

Annie held up a hand to stop Rose.

"Wait," she said. "Do I really need to be hearing this just before I start working with him?"

"Yes!" Rose said. "You need to have all your wits about you if you're going to be working with him."

The wink Rose gave her made Annie cringe.

"What?" Annie said, really wishing she had shut this conversation down before it had got started. "It's work. He asked for my help, he'll get my help. Nothing more, nothing less. There's a missing girl here, Rose."

Rose looked confused. "But you've *met* him."

"Look, he might be easy on the eye, but that doesn't mean I'm going to sleep with him."

"What a waste." Rose looked put out. She slumped onto the table and sipped at her champagne.

Annie felt her heart race at the thought of sharing her life with anyone. How could she even begin to explain her living situation, for starters? No. That would never do.

"Am I interrupting?"

Annie's head swung to the propped-open fire door and her stomach dropped into her shoes — Joe Swift was standing there in all his suited glory.

"Not at all," Rose said perkily, as she stood up. "Be my guest, I was just about to go and mingle anyway." She sailed off, with a none-too-subtle grin at Annie.

Annie was left with the awkward feeling that Swift had heard everything she just said. He took the space vacated by Rose and looked Annie square in the eye.

"Hello again," Annie said.

"Annie." Joe looked exhausted, the tiny lines around his red eyes telling their own story. "Do you have a car?"

She nodded.

"Pick me up from the station at eight tomorrow. We're going to meet Maggie Finch."

"Right, okay," Annie said, hesitantly.

"I hate these things," Swift added, nodding to the conference room, which was now full of their colleagues. For a moment, he seemed more human, less like a DI with the weight of a missing girl on his shoulders. "Is that why you're hiding out here?"

"Kind of," Annie said, thinking again of her conversation with Rose. "But Marion is already on the warpath. She's pissed at me for working with you, even though you're the one who asked me. So, I'd avoid her more than usual if I were you. She's after blood."

"I don't doubt it," he said, grinning. "She tried to pull strings higher up to stop me, but my plight was worthier than hers. You're obviously good at what you do; Marion was not letting you go easily."

Annie felt a swell of pride followed immediately by panic.

"I'm not *going* though am I? I mean, I'm still working with the probation service. I'm still a psychotherapist. This is just a one-off to help you out." No matter how much she said it, Annie couldn't help but feel a little like this shift was bigger than she had planned. Her excitement was unravelling.

"Yeah, we'll see, one case at a time, hey?" Swift said unhelpfully. "Shall we head in and see who else we can piss off? What with you defecting, and me being my usual self, I'm sure there are a few more feathers we can ruffle."

"I need my job, Swift," Annie said. "I'm not sure I should be fraternising with you if it's going to cause more trouble than it's worth."

Swift unfolded himself from the picnic bench and gave Annie a salute.

"Annie," he said as he stepped back into the hustle and bustle of the event. "It's always worth the trouble."

And with a wink he was gone.

FIVE

ANNIE ROLLED THE CAR INTO THE PARKING LOT AT THE back of the police station and turned off the engine. The sky was already bright blue above her, the air was thick, her back sticky. A promise of what was to come, as this summer had already been penned as the hottest on record. Only a scattering of protestors had littered the front of the building as Annie had driven past, half seven too early for most of them. Pulling into an empty space, Annie got out her phone and tapped out a text to Swift, grabbing his mobile number from his business card. She was early, stupid really given that her office-cum-flat was literally just around the corner, but the one-way system was more often than not at a standstill in the city centre and she wanted to make a good impression on her first day as a consultant to a detective. Especially as it could be her *only* day as a consultant to a detective.

She'd drifted off into a fitful sleep after ducking out of the networking event early the previous night. A sleep-addled, hangover brain would not do for this morning, Annie knew that. But she'd noticed the cold looks she was given by Marion as she'd gathered up her belongings and slipped out the door.

"You're early," Swift said as he pulled her passenger door open and folded his large frame into the battered old Golf. "Also, aren't you old enough to have an adult car yet?"

Annie gave him the side eye and turned over the engine.

"Good morning to you too, Swift. You're welcome for the lift," she said, taking the car back out onto the road and heading in the direction of the North Norfolk coast. "I don't see you offering to drive us to the very tip of the county in the middle of nowhere. And my car is *clean*, even if it is older than my career."

"Fair point," Swift conceded, looking at the pristine seats and floor.

"What time do you normally get into the office?" Annie asked, winding her window down and feeling the warm blast of air on her cheeks. "I could have picked you up from home, saved you the extra journey."

Swift gripped his bag on his knees as though someone was going to reach in his closed window and grab it out of his hands.

"No," he said shortly. "I'm always in the office."

They drove in silence for a while. Annie could feel Swift glance at her every now and again but she kept her eyes on the road. As the busy streets of the city gave way to the dual carriageway, she turned the radio down and wound up her window.

"You'll need to direct me from here, I'm not sure of the address," she said. "And it might also help if you can bring me up to speed on this case?"

Swift relaxed. He threw his seat back as far as it would

go, cranking the back down a notch as he unglued his knees from where they had been stuck together. He flipped open his bag and drew out a bunch of papers.

"Don't worry, just take this road as far as you can go without ending up in the North Sea; I'll direct you when we get nearer," he said, flicking through the pages. "Here it is."

He held up a photograph and Annie glanced at it for as long as she dared to without drifting over into the fast lane, or onto the grass verge. It showed a wooden front door, and from the quick glimpse she got at it, Annie could see it had once been blue. It looked old and worn; the paintwork peeled and cracked. There was something else…she couldn't quite figure out what, stuck to the door by the knocker.

"This is where we're going to," Swift said by means of explanation. "That's the Finches' front door. The house is pretty much on the same note. It's run down. Not just the decor either, the whole place felt neglected, dirty."

Annie nodded, taking in what Swift was telling her and trying to fit it around Tim Barclay, the dad, the man she had worked with over the summer months. She could picture him in his jeans, never the smartest, but he had looked clean at least; except for the few occasions he'd been using. Annie had mentioned this to his parole officer, as drug use was a violation of his terms, but she wasn't sure what the outcome had been. Annie ran this all past Swift as she overtook a convoy of caravans heading towards the coast.

"He left them, though, didn't he?" Swift said, rolling up his shirt sleeves.

Annie nodded. "Yes, he left them in the middle of our time working together, about a month ago now. Maggie was pregnant, not sure if she still is or if she's had the baby, but he said he didn't want to be a burden to them anymore."

Annie sighed, remembering the hollow shell of Tim Barclay as he'd told her how he'd just packed up his bags and left, right in the middle of the day, while Maggie and Orla were out crabbing. How small and insignificant he had seemed, sitting on her comfy chair with a plastic cup of water shaking in his hands.

"Did he tell you where he was going? Where he was staying?"

Annie shook her head. "No."

"Okay, so this is what I couldn't talk to you about yesterday. Look at this one," Swift said, holding up another photograph. "Our guys think it's a sign of something more sinister, maybe voodoo or a cult."

This time, closer up, Annie could make out the grotesque figure of a corn doll nailed to the wooden door.

"What the heck?" she said, narrowly avoiding a speeding Audi.

She pulled the wheel back to the left lane and took another look. The doll looked crudely made, not like the ones she'd seen at school harvest festivals or craft fairs. The head was twisted from strands of golden corn and tied in shape with a necklace of gingham fabric. The skirt of the body was loose and flowing.

"Is this the *weird stuff* you were hinting at yesterday morning?" Annie asked, tearing her eyes back to the road, a chill creeping down her neck.

"Yep," Swift said, putting the papers back in his bag and throwing it on the backseat. "Whoever took Orla left this hammered into the front door. At least, that's what it looked like. Maggie had never seen it before, and that's not something you'd forget in a hurry."

"That's not the work of Tim Barclay," Annie said. "That's not the work of anyone who loved that girl, surely? Have you cross-checked the MO with other areas? That's quite a distinctive calling card."

"Yeah," Swift said, running his hands through his hair. "Nothing comes up on other abductions of minors. Nothing that matches exactly anyway. There were a handful of other pagan symbols over the last ten years that were similar; a Phobos and Eris, but they're Greek and different enough not to match."

"Hmm," Annie mused. "I don't know. It doesn't feel like a family member has done this. It feels like something far more sinister. The perpetrator must have planned this too. If you're going to do something like hammer a corn doll to a door, you come prepared. Is the doll representative of anything? What makes your guys think it's voodoo or a cult?"

"And that, Annie, is why I have brought you in."

Annie flicked her head towards Swift. "What?"

"Eyes on the road, please."

"I thought you brought me in because I know the father?" Annie said, her stomach knotting in fear. "So you could use my skills to get information out of the mother?"

"Well, yes I did," Swift started, but Annie wasn't listening, she couldn't tear her eyes from him as his words echoed emptily around the car.

"What the hell, Annie?" Swift shouted as the long low horn of an HGV sounded. "Watch the ROAD."

She jerked the wheel in time to avoid rear-ending the lorry and swerved out into the fast lane. Her heart hammered fast in her throat.

"I thought working in this sector would mean people were less interested in me and my life history!" she shouted, her hands gripped on the steering wheel. "Yet here you are, bringing me in on a case that has *everything* to do with my life history."

Swift started squirming in his seat, trying to get a hold on the conversation, but Annie was on a roll.

"No, don't! Don't you dare try and placate me with niceties about my work, how you brought me in because I'm good at what I do. Rose warned me about you, but I didn't listen because she said you'd just try and get me into bed. But, you know, what you've done is way worse than that! What do I know about satanic cults and voodoo kidnappers? I'm a psychotherapist who works with probationers to keep them on the straight and narrow. I am not my father!"

SIX

"WOAH, ANNIE," SWIFT STARED AT HER WIDE-EYED AS SHE caught her breath, her knuckles still white on the wheel. "I literally have no idea what you're talking about. Please."

Her heart rate running away like a steam train, Annie wound her window down as she pulled back in front of the lorry. The wind from the passing cars rocked her little Golf about like a boat on the ocean. Petrol fumes and dust flooded her senses, but Annie didn't notice.

Breathe, you idiot.

She took a moment to collect her thoughts.

"Annie?" Swift's voice sounded like it was coming from down a well. "Are you okay? Do you need to get out, because if you do you need to pull over in the next lay-by. I don't want a dead shrink as well as a missing child on my conscience."

With the last few words, Swift's voice returned loud and clear to Annie's ears.

"Sorry," she mumbled from under her hair. "Sorry. *Shit*. I just thought..."

Annie stole a glance at Swift. She could feel her

cheeks burning with the embarrassment of what she'd just done. Another articulated lorry swept past then, rocking the car harder than the others, and Swift grabbed hold of the door.

"Do you think you can tell me what just happened there?" He looked peaky; his tanned face now a shade of shiny grey. "I'm used to people freaking out on me. But to tell you the truth it's normally the criminals!"

Annie gave a chuckle, glad of Swift's attempt to break the awful tension that had grown thick in the car.

"Also," Swift said as Annie's heart rate returned to the same cruising speed she was now doing. "What did you mean about Rose? Did she really say I'd try and sleep with you?"

Oh God, did I really say that?

Annie felt her face heat again and was glad of the blast of wind still pummelling her cheeks.

"Jeez," Swift added. "Is that really what people think of me at the station?"

"I don't know if it's everyone," Annie said, trying not to think about how embarrassed she was. "Maybe just Rose."

"But I've never, ever said anything remotely like a come-on to her," Swift said, rubbing his face again.

"Yeah," Annie said, a smile creeping on to her face. "She's gutted about that, too."

Swift made a garbled noise that could have been words and Annie laughed.

"Right," he coughed, clearing his throat. "Anyway. Don't worry, Annie. I'm not like that. Besides, I'm married."

His words tailed off as he looked out of the window. Annie remembered what Rose had said about Swift's absent wife. She didn't know what to say now, so she kept quiet. The only noises were the rushing of the wind and the steady thump of tyres on tarmac. They drove on for a while in silence. The road signs started to mention place names Annie knew were near the coast; Sheringham, Cromer.

"You wanna tell me what you meant back there about not being your father?" Swift said as Annie took the slip road down onto a single carriageway. "I honestly didn't mean to push any buttons. I just thought with your training in forensic psychology you might be able to help."

She chewed the inside of her cheek. Rumour had it that everyone knew about her past, but normally it didn't bother her because they were all too engrossed in their own lives to care about hers. And as long as her clients never found out, Annie was okay with it being out in the open. There had been a time, growing up, she would have been less relaxed about it, and that feeling had been reignited when Swift had shown her the photo of the corn doll.

"It's complicated," she said, her eyes fixed firmly on the road now, it was too winding to look away.

"I like complicated," Swift said. "That's why I'm a cop."

"Okay," she conceded. "My dad was a police officer himself, he seemed totally normal until one day he just upped and left my mum and me, I was only seventeen. He took my three-year-old sister with him. I've not seen either of them since, neither has my mum."

"That's awful," Swift said, and Annie could feel his eyes on her, she could feel the pity even though she couldn't see him. It was the reaction of everyone she told. Pity for Annie for being left behind. Pity for her for her missing sister and father. But Annie never felt sorry for herself, not in public anyway.

"Truly awful." Swift continued. "But what was it about voodoo and that weird doll that triggered your response?"

"My dad didn't just take my sister away with him to a new life. He joined a cult. A weird religious cult like the Jesus Army or the Solar Temple. But his was a neo-pagan group up north who facilitated altered state rituals and shite like that. For all I know, Mim has had her organs sacrificed to their gods." Annie puffed out a dry laugh. "I look for her every time I'm out of the flat. But I have no idea what she even looks like now. People know about it, it was big news at the time, but I work in this field because probation sends up so much weird shit that mine seems almost normal. I just assumed, when you showed me that photo, that you were working with me because of an insider's knowledge of the occult that I don't actually have. I don't. I really don't. But it was wrong of me to assume."

"Sorry, Annie," Swift said, his whole body facing her now. "I had no idea."

———

THE HOUSE LOOKED LESS WELCOMING than even the photo had portrayed. The North Sea was fast approaching over the flats of the marshes, and each wave sent up a spray of cold salty fingers as Annie drew herself out of the Golf. It was in stark contrast to its neighbour, whose path was well tended, bright with flowers that belied the harsh environment. Weeds caught at Annie's ankles as she followed Swift up the driveway to the door, where he knocked loudly on the flaking paint. The windows were darkened by what looked like years of dust and grime, but Annie could make out movement in one of the rooms. A shadow of a looming figure stooped at the door and it was dragged open by the shell of a woman that Annie barely recognised.

"Miss Finch," Swift said, standing to the side so Annie was in view. "DI Swift, we met on Monday, and this is my colleague Annie O'Malley. Can we come in?"

"Is there any news?" Maggie Finch looked like the North Sea had already swept her away.

"We're doing everything we can to bring Orla back safely." Swift was diplomatic, but Annie watched the mother shrink even more at his words.

They followed her through a small hallway to the front room which could have been either the dining room or the living room given the array of furniture. Though there was a general feeling of neglect—the dirt, the scuffed paint-work, the general cloying smell of bodies—Annie couldn't help but notice the small things. There were pictures of Orla dotted about the room, her young face smiling up at the camera. Some pieces of furniture looked like Maggie had upcycled them herself. There was a new rug in the middle of the room. It all made Annie think that perhaps the neglect wasn't Maggie's fault, but the result of a money-grabbing landlord. She made a mental note to speak to Swift about the ownership of the house.

Maggie Finch sat down on a dining chair with the weight of the world on top of her, heavier still with a baby bump that looked more than imminent. She pointed at the old worn sofa.

"Please take a seat," she said, her voice small.

Annie caught Swift wrinkle his nose at the sight of the sofa, but it looked clean, if a little worn to the springs. She sat down, thanking Maggie, trying not to wince at the pain

41

in her backside as she hit the wooden structure through the foam. Swift started pacing the room before deciding to lean against the window frame, silhouetted by the blue sky turned grey through the coated glass.

"As DI Swift said, my name is Annie O'Malley. I'm a psychotherapist. We have met before, do you remember me?" Annie said.

Then the door to the living room darkened with an approaching figure as a fierce rattle rang out.

SEVEN

A PLUMP WOMAN WITH AN APRON AND A TRAY FULL OF cups smiled at them all from the doorway.

"Sorry to startle you all," she said, in a sing-song York-shire accent. "I've made us all some tea. Thought we could use it."

She placed the tray on the dining table and pulled out another chair to sit on. She put a hand on Maggie's arm.

"This is Aila," Maggie said, clutching at Aila's hand on her arm, her face lit up in the presence of the motherly figure.

"Aila Clough," Aila said, pulling herself back to her feet with the help of the table. She reached out to shake Annie's hand. "Nice to meet you. I'm Maggie's advocate, she called and asked me to be here for when you arrived."

Advocate?

Aila groaned as she stood up straighter and walked over to shake Swift's hand. She was early fifties if Annie's guess was right; the woman reminded her of jam sandwiches and hot cocoa.

"Can I ask why you have an advocate?" Annie said, as they all sat back down.

"She was assigned to me by the County Council when Orla was given a social worker." Maggie looked pointedly at Annie. "I do remember you now. You worked with Tim, didn't you?"

Annie nodded. "Yes, I did. Tim was my client up until the week he disappeared. He missed his last session, which I thought was odd for him."

Maggie scoffed. "He's a waste of space. Look at me. How could he just desert me like this? *He* was the reason Orla was given a social worker in the first place, the reason I needed Aila here to be my advocate. And thank goodness, hey? Social services were worried about the access Orla may have to drugs, and the kinds of people that Tim used to be involved with. And they were right to be worried, weren't they? He's probably still involved with them, isn't he? They were worried he would hurt her. He hasn't just hurt her; he's hurting me too, and his unborn child. This must have been what he wanted."

She spat out the words, giving Annie a glimpse of how angry she was.

"You think that Orla's father had something to do with her disappearance?" Annie asked, nodding a thanks as Aila passed her a cup of tea.

"Of course he did," Maggie said, her anger swelling her like a balloon. "You saw him when he was using, he was a mess. He would do anything for a fix. *Anything.*"

"But what about the corn doll nailed to the door? Would Tim do that? Why would he do that?" Annie asked in a way that she hoped would keep Maggie's anger simmering and not boiling over.

Maggie's shoulders slumped and Aila put an arm around her.

"I don't know," she said in barely a whisper. "Maybe he was trying to scare me off? To warn me?"

"To warn you of what?"

"I don't *know*!" Maggie shouted. "Look, I'm holding on to the fact that Tim has Orla, because the alternative is something I *cannot* bear to think about. At least I know Tim. No matter what a mess he is, I know he loves and cares about Orla."

This was too much for Maggie. Her body crumpled into Aila's, wracked with sobs.

Annie looked over at Swift and nodded towards the door.

"Do you mind if we take a look in Orla's room again?" Swift said. Annie was on her feet in an instant.

It was hard to see as Maggie was enclosed in Aila's arms, but she shook her head. Annie and Swift left the room and headed up the rickety staircase. Annie could hear Aila's comforting words to Maggie but couldn't help thinking that they were empty words. Aila had no idea if the police were going to bring Orla home safely. Or even that Orla was okay. She probably thought she was doing the right thing, but false hope was sometimes the worst kind.

"Any idea who owns this house, Swift?" Annie said, rattling at the bannister as it came perilously close to falling free from the wall.

"Landlord," Swift said, already at the top and walking to the end of the landing. "We're trying to locate him; the letting agency is based in the city and they look after a few houses owned by the guy. They're sending over his home address, but I think he's in London. I hope they're not all as decrepit as this one."

Annie skipped a few steps to catch up.

"This place needs renovating. I don't think it's Maggie's fault her house is like this. She's looks like she's trying her best. Tim used to say she was the best mother."

"Tim is a drug addict who may or may not have snatched his own child weeks after abandoning her with tales of woe is me," Swift said bluntly, as he pushed open the door at the end of the landing. "Why are you so quick to defend Maggie? Don't advocates only get assigned to people that need parenting help?"

Annie shrugged. She knew Swift was right, but Maggie looked like a mother in distress. They walked together into Orla's bedroom. Light streamed in through the window, highlighting how sparse the room was, just an old, child-sized bed and a hanging clothes rail. The carpet was thin, the floorboards peeking through in places, white matting in others. A few teddies were scattered on the unmade bed and the clothes that had made it back onto the hangers were threadbare and faded. Annie's heart hurt at the sight.

"Oh God," she said, picking up a small rabbit with a blanket that may have at one time been pink. "This is why I don't work in Children's Services. It's too hard."

Swift followed her in.

"I know what you mean. People say you get used to it. That's bollocks. You never get used to something like this." He was looking around the small space, his eyebrows knotted. "What are we missing? Children are very rarely taken by someone they don't know. Orla is just about old enough to know about stranger danger. But it doesn't feel like the work of the father. What am I missing, Annie?"

Annie turned to Swift, his face was twisted. Her eyes locked with his. She could practically hear his words. Not wanting to look away, she walked up to him in the few steps it took and handed him the bunny, holding his hands as he took it for just a fraction of a second. Grounding him.

"I think your men may have been on to something," she said, quietly pushing shut the door to Orla's room, trapping their voices inside. "This doesn't feel right. I'm no expert, I'm not even a cop, but something about this has the hairs on the back of my neck standing on end."

"Your intuition is what makes you a great therapist, so I'm told. Keep talking."

They were both talking in whispers now.

"Was this room searched?" Annie asked, something niggling at her brain, but she couldn't quite put her finger on it.

Swift nodded. "Yeah, but there wasn't a lot to go on, as you can see."

"And is Maggie the religious type? Any affiliations?"

"Not that she said. Atheist, apparently."

"No. Tim wasn't either. Or he never mentioned it, and normally my clients with religious beliefs like to include them in their goal setting." Annie took a deep breath, her eyes still on Swift's. "Are there any known affiliations around here?"

Swift cleared his throat and looked away.

"I've got the guys on it back at the station," he said, stroking the stubble on his chin.

She shook her head and walked over towards the window. Swift closed the space between them.

"Annie," he whispered. "I'm really sorry. I never would have asked you to be involved if I'd known your family connections."

"It's okay," she said, feeling her neck prickle with goosebumps.

They stood next to each other, staring out at the blue skies and the fields behind the house. A flock of seagulls scattered about the sky, crying to each other with soulful, haunting screeches. The small patch of garden was as overgrown as the front had been. The fence was missing panels and toppling over into the neighbour's neat square of grass. They'd propped it up with some posts, but Annie could imagine they weren't happy about it.

"What about the neighbours?" Annie asked, curiously.

"An older couple. In their seventies. Unlikely suspects, they were both in the house when Orla went missing, but neither of them saw anything. And they're the only neighbours for miles around."

"Did they hear anything unusual?"

Swift shook his head and Annie let out a huge sigh, steaming the window with her breath. A smudge appeared under the steam and Annie's brain shot into gear.

"Swift," she said, standing back from the window. "Did your men clean this?"

"The window?" he said. "No, why?"

"It's clean, we can see out of it. I think it's the only window in the house that's not covered in a thick layer of greasy dust."

Annie stepped back towards the window and let out a long breath on the glass, moving her head around so she covered a whole pane.

"Shit!" Swift said, standing back to take in what Annie had uncovered.

The windows were old wooden ones, the kind children draw in pencil pictures of neat square houses. The pane at the top right was steamed up with Annie's breath, except for an outline of a large five-pointed star enclosed in a perfect circle, emerging like a ghost. Annie drew a breath and tried the other panes, her head swimming with the oxygen and the terrifying thought that this was looking more sinister than a familial abduction. The other top pane gave away nothing, and the bottom right was clear too. With her last breath Annie tried the final pane, her hand on the wooden windowsill to steady her swaying. Something was there. She breathed harder and stood back to see what she'd revealed.

"A triquetra," she whispered.

"A what?" Swift hissed.

"A Trinity symbol; you know, The Father, The Son, and the Holy Ghost? It's a Christian symbol of one Godhead, of power over all."

"And the star?" Swift asked.

"That's the sign of the devil."

EIGHT

"I don't know what they are." Maggie Finch grabbed Annie's phone and held it close to her face, staring at the photograph of the window Annie had taken. "Oh God."

She fell back onto the dining room chair, the legs creaking loudly in protest. Aila comforted the woman as she collapsed in on herself like a popped balloon. Tears streamed down her cheeks as she passed Annie back her phone.

"You've never seen them on her window before? Never seen them drawn anywhere else?" Swift asked, taking time to look around the living room.

"Never," Maggie sobbed. "What do they mean? Who's got my baby?"

Annie felt like her heart was being ripped in two. She had to get out of the room before she broke down herself.

"Excuse me." Ignoring Swift as he stared at her, Annie retreated back through to the hallway, trying to practice the deep breathing techniques she used with her patients.

She made her way through to the back of the house and

a room that once would have been a beautiful fisherman's kitchen. Now, like the rest of the house, it was coated in a layer of grease and grime. The once practical Aga had been replaced with an electric oven from the seventies and the tiles could have been any colour.

Annie went straight to the back door, flicked the locked hook out of its findings, and flung it open. Though the air was like walking into an oven, it was a darn sight clearer than the air in the house. The seagulls chattered in the blue overhead. Stepping outside, she looked up at the clear sky and took some deep breaths.

"Everything alright there, missy?"

The deep local accent startled Annie into fight or flight mode and her heart thumped in her chest. All the training she had completed to work in probation; the personal safety training, how to get out of a choke hold, how to manage in volatile situations…gone. All gone. If she was pressed on how to de-escalate an angered client right now, she'd be stumped. And for the first time, Annie wondered what the hell she was doing here in a missing girl's house, masquerading as someone who had any idea of what they were doing.

"Sorry, didn't mean to make you jump. Awful thing isn't it? Poor little Orla." A head popped over the garden fence. It belonged to a grey-haired old man, who looked as though he'd spent all his years looking head-long into the salt water spray from the sea.

Annie stepped through the weeds towards the fence that separated the two gardens, being careful to avoid the nettles.

"Hi," she said, waving in lieu of not being able to offer her hand. "Do you know the family well? I'm Annie, by the way."

"Harold Bishop," the old man said. "You with the police?"

"Yeah." It wasn't exactly a lie.

Harold nodded.

"I know them to say hi to. Lovely little girl is Orla, so sweet. Very talkative. I sometimes wonder how her mum copes with the non-stop chatter. But it's nice having a bit of life around here, you know what I mean? The wife and I aren't exactly spring chickens."

Annie nodded, she knew exactly what he meant. The area felt bleak and vast. With only the two houses, she imagined it could get very lonely out here.

"How long have they lived here?" she asked, kicking some more weeds out of the way so she could lean her arms on the rickety fence.

"'Bout two years I think," Harold said. "Give or take."

"And do you know why they moved out here?"

"Maggie told me once it was because of Tim's job," Harold said, his hand stroking the raspy stubble on his chin. "But Tim told me otherwise. I haven't seen him around for a while, he must be offshore again at the moment?"

Annie squinted at the sun. "What did Tim say?" she asked, ignoring Harold's probing question about Tim's whereabouts.

"He said he needed to get away from where he used to live because he didn't trust himself with the drugs. He was in with a bad crowd, was Tim. He thought Orla and Maggie were going to be his new start. And with the new baby coming, it looked like it might have been. But then he got himself banged up in prison."

Annie backtracked Harold a little.

"You said Tim wanted to get away from where he used to live because he didn't trust himself there?"

Harold grunted in agreement. "Said there were people there who would turn him back to his old ways. I think he was talking about drugs, he's got that look about him. Skinny chap. Very sunken eyes. But maybe that's me being judgemental."

Annie held off confirming his suspicions. It wasn't up to her to tell the neighbours about Tim's past. Not when Tim had divulged so much to them already.

"Did he say where that was? Where he was escaping from?"

"Ipswich." Harold spat it out as though it was a rotten fruit.

Annie gave him a look.

"My blood runs yellow and green. I can't say the word without saying it like that!"

Football!!

Annie laughed. She thought she'd better stop quizzing Harold now, or she might get into trouble with Swift. But one little thing was playing on her mind, so she pressed on, ignoring the voice in her head screaming at her to stop.

"The day Orla went missing, my boss said you and your wife were indoors?" she asked.

"Uh huh," Harold agreed. "Yup, we were watching *Homes under the Hammer*. It's got Dion Dublin in it now, ex-Norwich City player. I like to watch him looking around the awful houses to see if he can hide his disgust."

"Okay," Annie went on, feeling a trickle of sweat run down between her shoulder blades. "If you don't mind me saying, Harold, your hearing is perfect. Is your wife's just the same?"

Harold laughed. "Hers is better than mine. She can

53

hear me open the biscuit tin from the bottom of the garden."

"So, you're not one of those couples who has the television up really loudly?"

"Nope, not us."

"And you didn't hear anything?"

Harold's eyebrows knotted together.

"No," he said, his tone changed. "I told the police that. If we had seen or heard anything we would have helped. It breaks my heart what's happened."

"I know you would have, Harold," she said. "We're doing our best to bring her home."

Annie had reacquainted herself with the lingo faster than she imagined she would. But it wasn't any easier to say than it was to hear.

"Last thing," she added, shifting her weight off the fence and back onto her feet. "Did you ever notice anyone else hanging around? Anyone you didn't recognise. Or anything weird that made you double take or question what it was?"

Harold's face softened. He stood back from the fence too, treading carefully over the bright blooms he had covering the borders, and wiping the beads of sweat lining his forehead with a handkerchief from his top pocket.

"Now that's a very interesting question, young Annie," he said, smiling, studying her face. The hairs on Annie's arms stood to attention. "There haven't been any unknown visitors recently, not that I am aware of. We don't get many people around here. Normally it's just people passing from one posh coastal village to the next. They don't stop and admire the inconvenient blot on their landscape all that often."

Annie thanked Harold and hoped she hadn't overstepped the mark with her questions. As she picked her way over the knee-high grass to the back door, Harold leant over the fence and called out one last thing to her.

"Have a look at the post though, Annie," he said. "Your question just reminded me that I saw a young man out delivering leaflets not that long ago. We don't get leaflets around here because only the postman can normally be bothered to stop, and that's only because it's his job."

"Thanks, Harold," Annie waved, taking out her phone and jotting in the notes what he'd told her, so she could go over it with Swift when he'd finished with Maggie.

Steeling herself for what was going on inside the house, Annie stepped back in, enjoying the shade of the kitchen for a beat despite the stuffiness. Annie could hear the low rumble of Swift, and the rhythmic crying of Maggie, carried through the walls from the living room. The shrill of a phone cut through the sounds and Annie heard Swift excuse himself. He came into the kitchen, his phone by his ear as he barked his name into it.

Annie left him to it and went back through to the living room. Maggie wept gently into a tissue that was disintegrating in her hands, while specks stuck to her fingers and around her nose. Aila poured herself another cup of tea.

"Maggie," Annie said gently, going to sit back on the sofa. "Can you tell me where you keep your post?"

"In the box on the wall in the hallway." Maggie nodded her head in the general direction of the front door.

Aila sipped her tea and rubbed at Maggie's back.

"Do you want me to show you, love?" she asked Annie.

Annie shook her head; she didn't want Maggie to be left on her own in the state she was in. As it was the box was easy to find, hanging off the plasterwork by a nail that wasn't quite flush to the wall. Lifting out the piles of post and paper, Annie started to rifle through it. There were bills, more bills, red-topped letters from the gas company, pencil drawings of houses and cats, and envelopes that were still unopened from Norfolk County Council. About halfway through the pile, a lone leaflet almost fell to the floor. Annie pulled it out and put the rest of the mail back where she found it.

It was pretty nondescript. A5, white background, a single figure of an angel rising from a wave of water. She turned it over in her hands, sweat forming on her palms and sticking to the glossy picture. On the back it simply stated 'Angels of the Water', with an address that was a bit further up the coast. She took it back through to Maggie.

"What do you know about this place?" she asked, proffering Maggie the flyer.

Maggie took it with a shaking hand, turning it over once, twice, shaking her head.

"Nothing," she said, handing it to Aila's outstretched hand.

"It's one of those new-fangled churches," Aila said, giving the flyer back to Annie with a scowl. "They think they can come along and change God's word. I don't know what kind of upbringing these people had but I pray for them, and all the other heathens, every night. There's something not quite right about those people."

Maggie nodded at Aila's words. "Heathens," she said, dabbing at her nose with what was left of the tissue.

"O'Malley?" Swift was back in the room. "We need to get going."

He addressed Maggie and Aila as Annie gathered herself to leave. "Thanks so much for your time. Please know that we really are doing our best to bring Orla home. A family liaison officer will be with you in the next hour. You have my number, call me if you hear anything."

Swift bustled Annie along and they headed out the front door. Annie turned back, about to tell Swift everything she had learned while she had been there. She was proud of herself for the information she had and only a little nervous that she had overstepped every boundary that was in place to protect the public from a psychotherapist acting as detective. But before she could get a word out, Swift had bundled her in the car.

"There's been another abduction," he said, and Annie's blood ran cold.

NINE

ANNIE HUNG ON TO THE HANDLE ABOVE THE CAR DOOR FOR dear life as Swift took the winding country lanes faster than she normally took the motorway. He'd taken the driver's seat without being asked and Annie hadn't argued. Now she just feared for the paintwork of her trusty Golf.

Another missing child?

What did it mean? Where were they going? Annie had no idea if she should even be in the car anymore, a new case was very different to a two-day-old case where she knew the possible suspect. She felt in the way already.

"Do you want to drop me at home?" she asked, squealing a little as Swift took them out onto the dual carriageway of the bypass around the city.

"There's no time," he said, undertaking a BMW whose driver's salute told them exactly what he thought about that.

Annie felt a rush of excitement. Her skin rippled as Swift pushed his foot further down on the accelerator. Soon they were taking the slip road south of the city, heading towards a large, new build estate on the edge of a village that used to be further away from Norwich. A row of police cars lined the pavement of one of the identikit roads. Swift turned the car and pulled into the driveway of a semi-detached with a neat front garden. He barked instructions at Annie.

"You have two choices," he said. "You can stay in the car, or you can come in and keep your mouth shut."

Annie was out of the car before he'd even stopped talking.

Tammy Carter answered the door before Swift had even rung the bell. Dressed in a Kappa tracksuit, with her hair scraped back and gelled down, she looked no older than a teenager herself. Annie followed Swift and Tammy Carter into the house as the woman lit a cigarette. From the smell, Tammy had a forty-a-day habit that she liked to mask with supermarket plug-ins. Annie gagged and stood as close to the open window in the lounge as she could. The room was magnolia, with a feature wall of large pink flowers. Two pristine leather sofas sat at right angles, but Tammy wasn't sitting down, nor had she offered her two visitors a seat. A giant television took up most of the wall where Annie thought a fireplace might have been and it blazed out a bright but silent newsreel. There were silver photo frames dotted around the room and a slight, blonde-haired girl smiled cautiously out from them all.

Annie's instinct to make people feel at ease by asking the first question almost caught her out. But Swift was in there and making his own mark before the tension in the room was as thick as the cigarette smoke.

"Our foot patrol is out there now, doing door-to-door and searching the area," he said, and Annie could see his face go pink with the lack of oxygen as he spoke. "Could you tell us a little bit more about what happened? What time did Jodie go missing? Was she with you? Anyone else around?"

Tammy Carter looked like a rabbit in the headlights as she took in Swift's questions.

"How old is Jodie?" Annie asked, unable to help herself as she picked up one of the framed photos, ignoring Swift's death stare.

"Nearly four," Tammy replied, looking relieved. "She's a little shit quite a lot, but I love her. Terrible twos carry on until they're adults, I suppose."

Annie's poker face was working overtime, the millions of hours she'd spent biting back the eye-rolls was paying off. "And when did you notice she was missing?"

Tammy bit her lip and looked down at the immaculate vinyl floor that was supposed to depict wooden floorboards.

"I guess it was maybe a bit after lunch," she said, taking a long drag on her cigarette, her fingers shaking.

"And when did you last see Jodie?" Annie was on a roll now, she had completely forgotten Swift was there and that she wasn't supposed to be talking.

If Tammy could flush through her vapid skin, Annie imagined the girl's face to be bright pink.

"Probably about breakfast time."

Swift cleared his throat and the two women looked at him as if they were wondering why he was there.

"Breakfast time, probably?" he asked, unable to contain his own judgment.

"Well, yeah," Tammy continued, the end of her cigarette burning red in her mouth. "She brought me up a glass of water at about ten. Well trained, that one."

She gave a half laugh, half sob, then hacked up her lungs for a moment. Swift took the opportunity to give

Annie a look that could send her back to the car if she was less thick-skinned.

"And before that?" he probed.

Tammy shook her head sadly. "Dunno, I was asleep. But she normally gets herself up and watches cartoons until coffee time."

"And where is Jodie's dad, Mrs Carter?"

"It's Miss, I'm not married." Tammy stubbed her cigarette out on a crystal ashtray then immediately took it out of the room.

"What're you doing?" Swift hissed at Annie, but Tammy was back in the room before she had the chance to reply. The ashtray was sparkling again and a new cigarette hung from Tammy's lips.

"Jodie's dad could be anywhere by now," Tammy said. "He was probably a waster I met in a club, or someone I knew through friends, I don't bloody know. Whoever it was didn't even know I was pregnant, so there's not a chance her dad has anything to do with her vanishing—" She broke off and fell silent.

"Are there any friends that Jodie might have gone to visit on the estate? Does she have family close by she could walk to?"

Tammy looked as though Swift had just asked for one of her kidneys. "Jodie knows not to leave the house without me. And I've called all of my family, what do you think I am, a monster?"

"Well," Swift started to say, and Annie interrupted, not quite sure of where Swift was going to take his answer.

"What family do you have nearby, Tammy?" she asked.

"Me mum," she said, grimacing. "She lives in the next

61

estate over, moved here after I did. She likes to be close to me."

"And you've spoken to her already?" Annie asked.

Tammy nodded and Swift moved so he was standing in between Annie and her quarry.

"We've had our officers speak to your mum too, she was out at the bookies from nine this morning. Hasn't seen young Jodie."

Tammy nodded again and her face crumpled, white as a sheet. Annie thought that the amount of nicotine cursing around Tammy's body right now probably wasn't helping, but she guided the young mother down to one of the pristine sofas and sat holding her free hand.

"We're going to do everything we can to bring Jodie back to you, Tammy," she said, trying to breathe out the side of her mouth. "Can we have permission to go and look at Jodie's room?"

Tears trickled down Tammy's cheeks and fizzed onto the cigarette.

"Yeah, okay," she sniffed. "It's up the stairs, first door on the right. Be careful, she has more teddies than we know what to do with."

Swift was out of the room and halfway up the stairs by the time Annie had extracted herself from Tammy's side. She skipped up the last few stairs and was right behind him when he pushed open the door from a landing that was as clean and sparkling as the rest of the house.

Jodie's room was the epitome of girliness. As though someone had set off a bomb filled with pink and glitter and fluff and it had exploded, covering the walls. The bed was in the shape of a princess crown, the bedding dotted with what looked like matching crystal crowns sewn into a hot pink poly-mix. The white-cream carpet felt squidgy underfoot, a huge, heart-shaped, hot pink rug right in the centre of the room. A wardrobe was bursting from the seams with pink clothes of all shapes and sizes.

It was the total opposite to Orla Finch's room, yet Annie felt less comfortable here.

"I don't get it, why are we here?" Annie asked Swift as he stood pulling on a pair of blue gloves and taking in the room in silence. "Kids must go missing a lot, this doesn't look as though it's the same MO as the Finch family. The set-up is totally different."

Swift shook his head as though he was trying to shake out Annie's voice, so she kept quiet and wandered over to the window, checking the squeaky-clean glass for etchings. There was nothing. Annie watched as Swift strode over to the girl's bed, throwing back the covers to reveal hot pink sheets.

"It's a rarer occurrence than TV would have you believe," Swift said, pulling open the wardrobe doors. "Children of this age don't tend to just vanish like this. We get first dibs as we're on a similar case."

"Right," Annie said, drawing out the vowel.

"But I'm with you on this one," he said. "It feels different, less voodoo-y. I'll bet you my monthly wages that Jodie Carter is wandering around the estate somewhere with an older friend."

Swift's radio crackled before Annie could reply. He barked into it and they both listened as the crackly voice of one of the officers searching the perimeter broke through the heavy plastic radio.

"Sir," it said. "You need to see this. We're at the front gate."

Annie turned back to the window and saw two uniformed officers standing just outside the small, Astro-

Turf front garden. One of them looked up and in his hand was a familiar doll, crudely twisted from golden stalks of corn. And from this angle, looking down on the path, Annie could see now, drawn in child's thick chalk, the outline of the triquetra staring up at her.

TEN

ANNIE TIPPED THE LAST OF THE WATER FROM HER BOTTLE into the plant pot and pulled out the bed from under the sofa. Tucking herself into her sleeping bag, she thought back to the events of the day and wondered how on earth she'd gone from normal everyday client meetings on Monday to racing around the Norfolk roads, investigating two missing girls two days later. Two *young* missing girls who were probably crying for their mums right now. The thought made Annie's eyes prick with tears.

She'd spent the evening watching as forensics had descended on Tammy Carter's house. They'd stormed in, covered from head to toe in white overalls, and picked the house apart. Tammy had been taken off in a cruiser, only dropping the cigarette from her mouth as the car had slid away. Sniffer dogs had been given free rein of the estate, their tails wagging as they sped around the pavements, circling out from the missing girl's bedroom.

Annie had studied the corn doll through the evidence bag, its gingham ribbon incongruent with the evilness of the twisted stalks.

Her mind buzzing, Annie hadn't been able to sleep when she'd finally driven home, dropping Swift at the station on the way. Instead, she'd lifted her laptop lid and started researching the symbols they'd found in Orla's bedroom. The significance of the corn dolls and the way their bodies were churned up into the fields to ensure that the crops prospered. Annie had shivered when she imagined the young girls, taken and used to prosper their abductors. She prayed that it wasn't the case.

She flicked the desk lamp off, shutting her eyes and trying to find anything remotely positive to focus on. With grim images of broken and bent dolls invading her mind, it was almost a relief when her phone began to vibrate loudly on the floor beside her, the screen illuminating the office ceiling, revealing telltale stains from the leak she'd had last year.

"Ugh, what now?" she said, sitting upright and flicking the light back on.

The screen flashed with Swift's number and she swiped to answer him.

"Yes?" she barked, slightly more annoyed than she meant to sound.

"Annie, are you awake still?"

"You're the detective, you work it out."

Swift laughed into her ear.

"Touché," he said. "Look, there's been a discovery. The woods behind the new builds, near to where Jodie Carter disappeared."

Annie was wide awake now. She drew a sharp breath, fearing the worst.

"Not that kind of discovery. We haven't found her yet. Dead or alive."

"Oh, thank God," Annie said, exhaling. "Well, I mean,

not thank God you haven't found her. Just, you know, I thought you meant…"

She trailed off. They both knew what she thought he meant.

"The team and I are heading out now. Shall I get you on the way?"

Annie looked down at her pyjama-clad body.

"Give me ten minutes."

"I'll give you five, I'm already outside."

Shit.

Six and a half minutes later, Annie was sitting in the passenger seat of Swift's 4x4 as he powered through the dead streets of Norwich.

"What's been found?" Annie asked, tying her hair back with the band she always kept around her wrist. Mostly for CBT pinging, but occasionally it came in useful for its given purpose.

"Some teens out drinking stumbled across a child's toy," Swift replied, indicating and taking a left. "They only called it in because they'd heard about Jodie. Whispers spread like wildfire around estates like the one where she lives."

"Is it hers?"

Swift nodded as he accelerated up the slip road and onto the dual carriageway. "Yeah, looks like it might be. The mother has confirmed it's a match for the cuddly toy Jodie carries with her everywhere. It's being sent for DNA as we speak."

"Oh God, poor girl," Annie said. "I still sleep with my cuddly toy from when I was a baby. I can't imagine how scared she must be without it."

There was a thick silence in the car, heavy with the weight of the unsaid. The longer the girls were missing, at their age, the less likely they were to still be alive. Annie knew that.

"So what are we doing now then?" she continued.

"Talking to the teens," Swift said. "The search team have spread out to include the part of the surrounding woods where they were drinking. Sounds like a regular spot for them, from what the team were saying. So there's not likely to be a lot of evidence left amongst the beer cans and cigarette butts."

"Why did you want me to come?" Annie asked, feeling sure that she'd stick out like a sore thumb when they got there.

"I want you to talk to the teens with me, gauge them. You're part of the investigation now and I need you to be up to date with all of our findings. There's no point being a part-timer." Swift turned to Annie and winked. "Plus, I enjoy your company."

Annie felt herself blush and was instantly glad of the darkness of the car.

"I'll try my best."

They drove in silence for a mile or so, the fields flashing by in a staccato of streetlights. Annie's breath frosted up the glass of the window and made her think back to Orla Finch's bedroom window. Why were the symbols drawn on it? Who did it? How had someone gotten into the girl's bedroom and done that without Maggie Finch noticing? The locks of the house weren't great. Annie wondered if the perpetrator had broken in while the young family were out. She was in the throes of asking Swift these questions when he broke the silence first.

"You live above your office, then?" he asked as he took the exit off the dual carriageway and headed to the estate. "That must be both brilliant for the commute and awful for the respite."

Annie laughed despite herself.

If only you knew, she thought.

"Yeah," she said, wanting to tell him the truth but deciding against it—it was more embarrassing than it was worth. "I worked crazy long hours before you hijacked me, it made sense. Now it seems I'm never going to be off duty."

"Welcome to the police force!"

THE GROUP of teenagers looked younger than Annie had been expecting. She had expected maybe eighteen, nineteen at a push. This lot looked like they were fresh out of primary school. The four of them huddled around the police cruisers, their arms wrapped around their bodies to stave off the kind of coldness that comes with a shock.

"Where are their parents?" Annie asked Swift as they made their way towards a couple of adults who were quite obviously, to Annie's eyes, police.

"They've been informed," Swift barked, and the two officers turned to face him and Annie.

Annie took that to mean they didn't care that their kids were now talking to the police and were happy to leave them to it.

"They're not under arrest, so they don't need an adult present, but you would have thought at least one set of parents would want to be there for them," Swift said, reading Annie's mind, or perhaps her face which was anything but a poker face. "Annie O'Malley, this is my team. Team, this is Annie."

"Hi," the woman stepped forwards first. Even in the

low light, Annie could see she had a peroxide blonde mop of chin-length hair and steely grey eyes. Though about a foot shorter than Annie, the officer gave no signs of being anything other than tough. "DS Belle Lock, but you can call me Tink, seeing as you're part of the inner circle now."

She held out a hand and Annie shook it.

"Despite the rest of the circle not being consulted!" the man added, stepping forward and offering his hand. He was tall, broad, and wouldn't look out of place in a bare-knuckle brawl. "Hi, I'm DC Tom Page."

Annie shook his proffered hand, slightly concerned about her own fingers.

Tink and Page. Annie tried to ingrain their names in her mind, the same way she'd learnt to memorise the names of clients.

"Right," Swift interrupted. "What and who have we got?"

"Come with me, Guv," Tink said. "And I'll introduce them."

"Guv?" Annie whispered to Swift. "I thought you said—"

Swift gave her a hard stare and Annie remembered where she was and why she was there. She reigned her hilarity in and followed the *Guv* as Tink led them over to the group of teenagers.

"Which one of you found the toy?" Swift barked.

Annie thought he was good at being ferocious when he needed to be, but this was not one of those times. A fleeting thought crossed her mind that perhaps he'd scared away all his police partners, which was why he now needed to rope in an outsider to help.

The teenagers shrunk a little under his stare. Annie stepped up.

"You're not in any trouble," she said, beginning to feel a little heady—the smell of weed coming from the youths was overwhelming. "We can think about overlooking the drugs if you can give us more information about the toy. What made you call the police, for starters?"

The smallest of the teens looked up from under his hood at Annie.

"That girl what went missing," he said, his voice barely broken. "She's the same age as my sister; my mum told me about what happened after she heard it from me nan down the shop. She said that girl's mum was an accident waiting to happen. Guys in and out all the time. Mum said my sister's not allowed out of her sight until whoever took that girl is caught. So, I thought the teddy might be important, you know, when I saw it. My sister's got one just like it, carries it around with her everywhere she goes."

"You were right to think it was important, that was quick thinking," Annie said, and the young boy beamed a smile at her as though praise was few and far between. "Can you show us exactly where it was when you found it?"

The boy turned to look at his mates, who were still focused solely on their state-of-the-art trainers.

"It was over there," the boy nodded towards a shabby-looking garden at the edge of the woods, the fence half falling over, and the ivy thicker than tree trunks in places. "Behind Old Man Dick's house."

That got a few sniggers from the rest of the teens.

"Old Man Dick?" Swift asked, his eyebrow raised. "Who's that when he's at home?"

"The weirdo who lives in that shit heap," the boy said, his chin raised towards Swift defiantly, as though waiting for retribution for swearing. "We're not allowed near his house, Mum says he's too fond of the kids, if you know what I mean?"

"Yes," Swift said. "We know what you mean. And that's why you're all hanging out at the back of his garden is it?"

"We're not scared of him!" One of the other teens piped up. "I could have him any day of the week."

"He wouldn't want you," the girl of the group added, laughing. "You're way too old."

Annie's senses were tingling somewhere at the back of her skull. She moved away from Swift and the teens and motioned to DS Lock.

"Is that true, Tink?" she asked her. "What they're saying about the man who lives there?"

Tink shook her head. "No. Richard Able has no rap sheet. It's a rumour started by bored kids and picked up by their even more bored parents."

Annie nodded a thanks and went back to the teens, who were now all joining in, chivvied on by their mutual love of ridiculing Richard Able.

"No rap sheet, Guv," Annie said quietly to Swift, who acknowledged her before he realised what she'd called him.

"Yeah," said the biggest teen, his hands low in his jeans pockets, his eyes dark with the effects of the weed. "My dad told me he's one of those weirdo cult people. It's a good way to get access to young kids though, isn't it? Through the church. Everyone knows it."

Abruptly, Swift stood up straighter and puffed out his chest, looming over the youth. "Wait," he said, his voice authoritative. "Let's backtrack a little, sonny. Part of *what* cult?"

The teen's eyes widened in fear. He looked like he was going to burst out crying.

"The angels one," he said quietly, his toe poking the earth. "You know?"

"Yes we do," Swift said, raising a hand to his team. "Thanks for your time. Now please can you all bugger off home to bed so I don't have to talk to your parents about that rubbish you've been smoking?"

The teens looked at each other with relief.

"Page!" Swift shouted across to Tom. "Find someone to make sure these kids all get home safe. Tink, go and find out who did door-to-door earlier, and why we're only just finding out about this." He turned back to Annie. "And you, come with me. We're going to pay this Old Man Dick a little visit."

FOR STARTERS, Old Man Dick was not old. The jury was still out on whether or not he was a dick. Annie looked around the house as he led them through to his living room. This estate was only ten years old. From the looks of his house, Richard Able had been here for the entirety of the ten years and never once thrown anything away. Newspapers were stacked to ceiling height along the hallway, carrier bags full of what looked like paperwork were shoved into any available gaps. The downstairs toilet door could not be closed due to the large armchair blocking its way.

They all squeezed past the obscure furniture, ending up in a room just as rammed as the hallway. A small, grease-stained gap on the sofa showed where Richard Able spent most of his days. He took a seat without offering one to Swift and Annie, not that there was anywhere else free—the rest of the chairs were covered in stacks of paper. A dusty old TV took up the majority of another armchair, and buckets containing dubious-looking fluids dotted the floor. The smell was making Annie's eyes water, but she couldn't see any sign of a window to stand beside—they were blocked out by the towers of newspapers.

"I'm not what they're saying I am," Richard Able said, shrugging in his sunken position on the sofa. 'Like I told your guys yesterday, I keep myself to myself mostly. Except for the church. My congregation understands me, you see."

"Your congregation?" Swift asked.

"Yes, I'm church leader of the South City branch of Angels of the Water."

"What does being a church leader involve?"

"Looking after my women however they need me, which is where I was when poor little Jodie was hurt. I told that to your officers yesterday too. My congregation will tell you the same. I'm a carer, not a destroyer. I'd have no reason to hurt a child."

"No one said anything about hurting a child, Mr Able," Swift said sharply. "We just want to know where she is."

"Taking a child from their parent *is* hurting it, DI Swift."

Annie noticed the calm and collected manner in which Richard Able spoke to Swift. She remembered back to her first meeting with him, how nervous she'd been, and she hadn't even been a suspect.

"Where do you hold your meetings, Mr Able?" she asked, looking around the room. "Not here?"

"They're not called meetings, dear," he replied, his

stare sending a shiver up Annie's back. "They're assemblies."

"Answer her question," Swift ordered.

Richard nodded, his movement slow and assured. He didn't seem at all thrown by Swift's orders, or by the presence of two strangers in his home.

"They're *obviously* not here," he said. "My house is sacred to me." His eyes ran up and down Annie in disgust. "I hold my assemblies in the South City branch church house. Not like some other branches, whose leaders use their houses for other means."

"Other means?" Swift asked.

"Yes."

Richard Able crossed his arms and kept his mouth shut, obviously he wasn't going to be forthcoming with information about what other means he was talking about.

"How many branches of the church are there, Mr Able?" Swift asked.

"Ten." Richard Able was being as insensitive as they come.

"Do you know the leader of the North Norfolk branch, Mr Able?" Annie asked, keen to find a connection

"Of course."

The room fell into a thick silence, all the ambient sounds were soaked up by the years of hoarded news.

"Mr Able." Swift was right up beside the man now. "Stop being so obtuse and answer the bloody questions."

Mr Able sat stock still for a moment, drumming a dirty nail on his thigh, then spoke. "The North Norfolk leader is a downright pompous man. He lives in Brancaster. His own house is bigger than the bloody church and that's no surprise given that he rents out his church house." Richard

Able cleared his throat and took a deep breath. "Sorry. Yes. His name is Peter Johnson."

Swift threw Annie a look. It was clear that something about Peter Johnson had rattled Richard Able's cool, calm exterior, and Annie knew that Swift had seen it too.

"Thank you for your time, Mr Able," Swift said. "We'll see ourselves out."

ELEVEN

Swift cleared the station car park bollards by millimetres and steered the 4x4 into an empty space. The sun was now high in the sky and having come straight from the woods, having had no sleep the previous night, Annie was struggling against the brightness. She followed Swift as he buzzed them both into the back doors of the station and through to reception. The usual gaggle of protestors hung around the entrance, and Annie saw a flash of a friendly face she recognised, probably from her probation work.

"Morning, Rose," Swift said, and Annie noticed his ears turning pink.

"Morning, Rose," she said herself, giving her friend a little wave.

Rose's eyebrows shot to the ceiling, but before Annie could explain that she and Swift had arrived together from a crime scene and not from his bedroom, Swift was through the inner sanctum entrance and the door was fast closing.

"This," he said, crashing open a pair of double doors to

reveal a large space buzzing with people, "is the centre of activity. He led her through another set of double doors to the incident room. "And this is our haven."

It could have been any of the conference rooms Annie had been in before, had it not been for the large notice-board taking up the majority of the far wall, heavy with pictures and notes. Annie had only ever seen incident rooms like this one on the television, and up until now the idea of a noticeboard covered in clues had been one of make-believe. She walked up to it and studied the pictures of the two missing children pinned at its heart. There were other faces she recognised dotted around the girls: Maggie Finch, Tammy Carter, Tim Barclay, and a couple of men she didn't recognise. DC Page came up behind Annie and pinned a new printout of Richard Able's face onto the board, on Jodie Carter's side.

"Get anything useful out of him?" Page asked, pressing the pin into the board harder than necessary.

Annie was primed to give Page the lowdown when Swift piped up loud enough to get the attention of the whole room.

"Listen up, everyone!" he yelled, clapping his hands together. The room descended into a hush and Swift opened his arms towards Annie. "For those who haven't met her yet, this is Annie O'Malley, she's working with us on the case. Annie worked with the father of Orla Finch before he went AWOL and I brought her in to tap into the relationship she has with Mrs Finch. It worked, and she's here for the duration of this case. Answer her questions and listen to what she has to say. She may be a psychother-apist but she's also a trained police officer."

Annie felt her cheeks heat as all eyes turned to her now. Two of the team she recognised from their brief introduction last night, but there were a few extras, PCs she guessed, who eyed her suspiciously. She lifted a hand to wave at them, then thought better of it.

"Hi," she said, steeling herself. "Nice to meet you all. I'm a psychotherapist, as DI Swift mentioned, but my policing career was short and a long time ago."

"Great, he's brought in a shrink," a voice whispered from the back of the room. Annie could just make out the snide smile of an older man with an unfortunate comb-over and a shirt struggling to stay buttoned. No one laughed at his joke but that didn't deter him. "I thought all that profiling bollocks was done with. What's she here to do, read our minds?"

"Yes," Annie said, louder now, addressing the man's concern. "PC…?"

The man flushed the same colour as Annie's tired eyes.

"PC Neil Bush," he said, sheepishly.

"Right then, PC Bush," Annie continued. "As you've already gathered, I'm here to read the minds of the many. So, I'd pipe down if I were you, or I might read yours, and I'm guessing it isn't pretty!"

Annie's hands were sweating, but from the laughs filling the room and the apoplectic look on PC Bush's face, she figured she had about gotten away with it. Swift was trying to conceal a laugh himself as he walked towards Annie and the noticeboard.

"Ouch," he mouthed to her, grinning, before spinning around and facing the room again, his face straight. "Right, Old Man Dick, aka Richard Able. I don't think he's our perp, but what do we have on him?"

Another PC, who was now distancing herself from a fuming PC Bush, stood up.

"PC Anderson, welcome to the team, Annie," she said,

before turning her attention to Swift. "Able's got an alibi, confirmed with the member of his church he was consoling, at the time we know Jodie Carter went missing."

"The whole time?" Swift asked, his head cocked. "That early in the morning?"

"Yeah," she replied. "Apparently the woman is newly divorced."

"Hmm," Swift said again.

Undeterred, the PC carried on. "He's certainly providing a service of some sort to his congregation."

"He told us he's the South City leader, that he has his own building to use for the church. How rich is this cult?" Annie asked the team.

"Very," DC Page answered. "To join the Angels of the Water you have to give them your worldly possessions. Not your house, or anything like that, but a generous percentage of your wages and any other donations can certainly help your standing in the community."

"We need to find out more about the North Norfolk church leader too, and what he does with his church-owned property," Annie continued. "What was his name again, Swift?"

A murmur rippled around the room.

"Peter Johnson," Swift said. "Bush, Anderson — you two get out to the coast, find out what you can on this Mr Johnson and the properties he owns."

The two PCs, Bush still looking somewhat pink, gathered their bags and coats and made their way out the door. The room quietened again and Swift addressed Annie.

"We'll head out there later, for now we need to look at what else we have."

Annie nodded and they both turned to the noticeboard.

"Apart from Orla's dad, Tim Barclay, do we have any

other offenders living local to either of the two girls?" she asked.

Annie could feel Swift's gaze on her but she focused on the pictures pinned to the blue fabric. She recognised Tim Barclay of course, even though the picture they had was an old one from his pre-prison days.

"Any suspects that knew both the families?" she added, looking at Maggie Finch's drawn features staring out at her from the board.

"You're sure you haven't done this before?" Swift asked. "You were only a PC for a few months, weren't you? Never a detective."

"I watch a lot of police drama on the TV," Annie replied. "It's not that hard really, is it? A few episodes of *Line of Duty* and *Marcella* and I'm pretty much up to speed."

She laughed, unsure that her humour would go down very well. Swift punched her gently on the shoulder.

"Oi," he fake gasped. "Watch it, or I'll lock you up and throw away the key."

They stared at each other for a moment.

"I learnt *that* on *The Bill*!" he added, smirking.

Though they were sharing a joke, the room felt full of the questions surrounding the missing toddlers. Annie dropped her smile and looked again at the board.

"So, who are our suspects?" she asked the detectives left in the room.

Tink stepped up to the board and pointed to the picture of Tim Barclay.

"First up we have Orla's father, he's AWOL, and he's a known offender." She moved her hand over Maggie's picture to the scribbled names of the Finches' neighbours. "We can rule out Mr and Mrs Bishop as searches came back clear. And the landlord of the Finches' house, as he lives in London and has an alibi."

Her finger slid back to the picture of Orla's mother. "Maggie Finch was given an advocate by the council because they were worried about her child, so Maggie herself isn't in the clear yet. She was the last one to see Orla, who's to say they weren't playing hide and seek at all?"

Tink moved slightly to Jodie Carter's side of the board. "We have no idea of the whereabouts, or the who-abouts, of Jodie's dad. We're on it though and will let you know as soon as we have anything, Guv." She tapped hard on the next picture. "Richard Able, aka Old Man Dick, has an alibi."

"But Angels of the Water has come up in both cases," Annie interrupted, holding her hands up as an apology. "The Finches' neighbour asked me to look through Maggie's post as he and his wife had recently been sent a flyer from their local branch. And Richard Able is a leader of the same church."

"It's the only thing linking them at the moment," Tink agreed.

"Don't forget we also have the dolls," Annie added. "They're occult; ground into the earth to provide prosperity for the farmers of years gone by. Could they be connected to the church?"

"And the signs drawn on Orla's window and Jodie's path," DC Page said. "They could be something similar? A ritual, maybe? Like the old Theobald case?"

Annie felt the temperature in the room drop a few degrees.

"Who's Theobald? What kind of ritual?" she asked, not really wanting to know the answer.

82

Swift stepped away from the board, running his hands through his hair. He let out a sigh and slumped into one of the chairs around the large table in the middle of the room. Tink and Page went to join him. Annie took a chair opposite Swift and waited until he'd lifted his head.

"Thomas Theobald was an old case," he started. "It's not him, he's going to rot in jail. And I didn't learn that from *The Bill*, that's just how we all feel. He was my first case as a uniformed officer. He was arrested fifteen years ago now, caught trying to leave the country with two babies he'd stolen from their parents. It was a huge operation. Theobald was being paid vast sums of money from an organisation in Europe that harvested and sold children's organs."

"What the fuck?" Annie blurted, unable to help herself.

"I know," Tink agreed, nodding grimly at her.

"It's very unusual for around here," Swift continued. "Something so callous and unthinkable. One of the kids was never found. His case is still open in the misper team, though it's a cold case now."

They all fell silent. Annie looked again at the pictures of the two missing toddlers.

"You think this may be related?" she asked them.

"We're hoping not," Page said, his young face looking browbeaten. "Because then those girls don't stand a chance. Orla's been missing for nearly sixty hours, and Jodie for over 24. Theobald had his children out of the country within a day."

"Were any pagan tokens or signs left in the cases of the Theobald children?" Annie asked.

Swift shook his head. "No. Nothing whatsoever. I don't think this is related; the children are older too. But it's bringing it all back, and I don't want anything to get

83

out in the media about how this case may be a repeat of the Theobald one. That's scaremongering we don't need right now."

They all nodded.

"I think our best bet right now is to look deeper at this so-called church; to go and see Peter Johnson and hear what he has to say; and to find Jodie Carter's dad and see if he has any links to Orla Finch." Swift stood up so suddenly that his chair wobbled precariously on two legs before settling again. "Page, get on to Miss Carter and find out who Jodie's dad is, or at least narrow it down to a few possibilities if she can. Tink, go and talk to other members of the South City congregation, see if you can get some more info about what the hell goes on at these Angels of the Waters' assemblies."

He lifted his chin at Annie, who stood up immediately.

"Annie," he said. "You're with me. I'm running on empty at the moment, so we'll take a detour through Maccy D's on the way out to the North Norfolk coast. I've got a feeling about this Peter Johnson and his church that is giving me the heebie-jeebies."

"Right, Guv," she said, smiling at his wince.

TWELVE

"I DIDN'T REALISE HOW HUNGRY I WAS," ANNIE SAID, swallowing the last of her sausage and egg muffin and peeling the lid from her coffee cup.

"I don't know about you," Swift replied, wiping his mouth with the back of his free hand, "but my brain doesn't work on an empty stomach." His other hand remained firmly on the steering wheel of the 4x4 as they flew along the dual carriageway, back out towards the coast.

"Mine's normally okay with caffeine and sleep," Annie said. "So this will have to suffice."

She held up the coffee cup until it sloshed dangerously close to the edge. And though Swift's car wasn't quite as pristine as her trusty Golf on the inside, it didn't warrant being covered in a Maccy D's flat white.

They trundled along the dual carriageway for a while, the only sound the thrumming of the wheels against the tarmac and the cars passing them on the fast lane at way over the speed limit. Annie fell into a daze as the rhythmic noise lulled her almost to sleep.

"So, how are you?" Swift asked, his voice jolting her so hard she had to grab the top of her takeaway cup to stop it flying over the dashboard.

He snorted. "Were you asleep?"

"I'm not used to missing whole nights! I'm not trained like you guys are. I haven't done two years of shift work. My clients all stick to the nine-to-five. You know, normal working hours." Annie opened her window and let the warm air hit her in the face.

"Sorry," Swift said, flicking the radio on. It started blaring out Classic FM. "What?" he said, as Annie raised an eyebrow at him. "I'm more refined than I look, you know."

"I didn't think you weren't...refined," Annie said then immediately regretted it. She cleared her throat. "Anyway, what were you saying when you woke me up?"

Swift was giving Annie the stare she'd seen him give Richard Able, and she didn't like it. She was supposed to be the one who could read minds, not him. She turned to study the airbag logo on the glove compartment instead.

"I was just wondering if you're okay?" he said, his eyes back on the road. "You know, with the whole church cult, missing kids thing. But particularly with the church cult. Given your history."

Annie considered her nails for a good few minutes before replying. She'd been so swept up in the tragedy of the missing toddlers that she hadn't given any thought to what exactly was happening, and how it might affect her, since the moment she almost killed herself and Swift on the road last time they were heading to the coast. Truth be told, she had no idea how she felt about the whole thing.

"Your well-being means a lot to me, O'Malley," Swift continued. "I don't want to be the bad guy who dragged you from a good job into a world of murk and murder and despair."

That made Annie laugh.

"There's no murder on the cards yet, Swift," she said. "And there's no despair from me." She took a breath and wound her window back up so she could hear herself talk. "You know, it's weird. I thought I'd be thinking about Dad and Mim all the time working with the police and this whole cult thing but being so involved in this case has actually taken my mind off them. Maybe it was what I needed all along? Not bloody government paperwork, but good old-fashioned police work. My job has been getting a bit tedious of late—don't mention a word of that to my lovely boss now, will you? Marion would string me up—and I think this is just what I needed. So thank you. Though, I'm obviously not happy about the missing girls. Do you think we'll get them back safely?"

Swift sucked air in through his teeth. He indicated, then took a left onto a smaller road that Annie recognised from their last trip.

"Normally I'd say it's unlikely after this long has passed," he said. "But I like to stay positive."

"Yeah," Annie said, staring out of the window and catching sight of the sea. "Yeah, me too."

PETER JOHNSON WAS NOT AT ALL how Annie had been imagining him. He was tall, well dressed, and annoyingly attractive. If it wasn't for that same air of importance that Richard Able had also exuded in abundance, Annie would have found herself falling for Peter's charm a little too easily. As it was, his pomposity stood out like a bad smell and Annie was quite happy to grimace instead of smile at him.

"I don't know what Richard has been saying about me, but I'll have you know everything I do is above board. Unlike him." Peter was pacing the room of his cottage, which overlooked the Staithe. It was decked out with brown leather and hard corners, so Annie guessed there was no Mrs Johnson.

"Care to elaborate on that, Mr Johnson?" Swift asked from his position by the window. Just over his shoulder, Annie could see sail boats toppled on their sides awaiting the rising tide.

"His congregation are nearly all single, and let's just say he helps them overcome their husbands, even if they don't need to." Peter sipped at an espresso from a white porcelain mug that had been filled by the snazziest coffee machine Annie had ever seen in a private home. This Johnson guy obviously had money.

Annie took a sip of her own coffee and felt the caffeine coursing through her bloodstream. Wincing, she tried to focus on what Peter Johnson was saying about Richard Able.

"I'm always there for my congregation, but I always keep my clothes on." The way his eyes were fixed firmly on Swift as he spoke made Annie wonder what lies he was telling. "Now, tell me Officers, how can I help you further than I already helped your colleagues earlier?"

"Detectives," Swift corrected; Annie didn't add her own correction. "And as far as I can see you weren't that forthcoming with information earlier either."

"They were questioning my integrity, *Detective*," Peter Johnson spat out in disgust. "There was really no need for that."

Annie watched as Swift pulled his shoulders back and grew a few inches.

"Mr Johnson, there are two missing toddlers, one of whom is from around here," he said. "We are doing our very best to bring them home safely and any help you can give us is greatly appreciated. Of course, we could have this conversation down at the station if that would make it easier for you to concentrate?"

That stopped Mr Johnson in his tracks.

"No," he said simply.

"Well then," Swift continued. "Can you please tell us a little more about the property you own as a perk of being a leader of the Angels?"

Annie saw a slight hesitation in Peter Johnson's movements. So slight it might not have happened; it was the flush creeping up his neck that gave him away.

"It's not an easy job, you know." He sounded defensive.

"You should try mine!" Swift replied, not having any of it.

Annie watched the exchange carefully, the creeping sensation that Peter Johnson was not being totally honest with them washing over her.

"How much do you get paid in this *difficult role?*" Swift asked.

"That's none of your business, Detective."

"And this property," Swift continued. "Where is it and what do you use yours for?"

Peter Johnson swallowed the last of his espresso, the tiny cup partially hiding his face momentarily, giving him a second's reprieve to think about what he was going to say.

"If you think I've got a secret harem of women in my

sacred church property, you'd be very much mistaken. Like I said, I'm not Richard Able."

Annie noticed his question avoidance. Seemingly, Swift did too.

"That's not what I asked." He sounded like he'd had enough of Peter Johnson. "Or do I need to get a warrant to look around the property? Because with missing kids, I can have one in a few hours."

Annie had no idea if this was true, but by the looks of it, neither did Mr Johnson.

"Look," he said, his shoulders sagging somewhat. "I don't use my church property for myself. I use it to help others. Any church work I do here. You can see for yourselves that it's a beautiful place, why would I need a new build stuck in the middle of an estate when I have this?"

Pompous and judgemental, Annie thought, putting her full cup down on the table with jittery hands.

"Please use a coaster," Peter Johnson said, not even looking in her direction.

She lifted the cup back up and bit her tongue.

Swift's patience was clearly not just running thin but was practically see-through. "So, what *do* you use your church property for?"

Mr Johnson cleared his throat and mirrored Swift's stance.

"I rent it out."

"And that's allowed on the terms of the agreement to you is it?" Annie asked.

Peter Johnson ignored her and directed his reply to Swift.

"We're allowed to use the properties to assist the church's responsibilities in any way we see fit."

Swift and Annie let the silence circle the air. Peter Johnson was the one to fill it.

"Look, these two men needed a place to live, so who was I to turn them down in the face of adversity?" He jutted his chin out in defence.

"So you're letting them stay there out of the goodness of your heart, are you?" Annie probed.

"Well, yes," Peter Johnson replied, looking Annie in the eye this time—she knew it meant he was lying.

"The goodness of your heart and how much rent per month, Mr Johnson?" she added.

"Look, what is this? I have nothing to do with those missing girls. So I make a little extra money on the side, sue me. It's not like the church needs it, and I am doing those *two men* a favour." He spat the words out with so much disgust that Annie couldn't help but question why.

"Who are they, Mr Johnson?" she asked. "And why did they need your help?"

His flush was full-on red this time, and Swift moved in for the kill.

"Do we need to get a warrant? What aren't you telling us?"

"No!" Mr Johnson shouted, before collecting himself enough to quieten down. "No, please. Look, the first guy came to me through the council. Said he needed a place to stay, to get clean. I thought that drugs were a vice before I joined Angels of the Water, but now I *know* they are the food of the devil. The second guy has only been there a few weeks. Needed a place to stay in an emergency. He found me through my first tenant."

"And you thought you'd offer the house as what, a rehab clinic?"

Mr Johnson gave Swift a withering look.

"I'd be charging a hell of a lot more than £600 a month each for a rehab clinic, I can tell you that for nothing."

"How generous," Swift said.

Annie couldn't work out if Swift meant the information or the rent. Around here, £600 wouldn't get you much above a bedsit, and it sounded like the church house was at least a whole house.

"So, who are they?" Annie asked.

"Pardon?" Johnson was really starting to get on her nerves now.

"The names of the two men you have living in your property. Who are they?"

Pete Johnson rubbed his face with his hand until his skin pinked. "The first guy is a Mr Grey Donovan."

"And the second, Mr Johnson," Annie probed, a cold feeling spreading in her gut. "Who is living there with Mr Donovan?"

Mr Johnson slumped down into the hard-looking leather chair. "It's Mr Barclay. Tim Barclay."

THIRTEEN

"WHY THE HELL DIDN'T HE TELL US THAT IN THE FIRST place?" Annie yelled over the sound of Swift's tyres screeching on the tarmac. "If he really has nothing to do with the missing girls, why not just tell us outright? He's shifty, that's for sure."

"Yep," Swift agreed, his full focus on the road as they sped along.

"It's too much of a coincidence. The corn dolls, the occult symbols, the connection with the church or the cult or whatever you want to call it. And now Tim being a lodger of Mr Johnson."

Swift took a sharp corner and Annie yelped, reaching for the handle above her head. They sped off down a lane so narrow that Annie was praying to a god she didn't believe in that they wouldn't meet another car travelling in the opposite direction.

"Aren't you supposed to have blues and twos for this kind of speed?" she cried as they approached cross-roads without much indication that they were going to slow down.

"Not when there's two children in danger," Swift said, his voice steady. "Besides, I've done extra training, so don't worry, you're perfectly safe."

Whether he was being facetious or not, Annie couldn't stop worrying as they sped over the junction and down another country lane. The grass was so overgrown on the banks at the side that she couldn't see anything past the windows, and the front wasn't much better. She contemplated closing her eyes but thought better of it as her stomach was already churning after that McDonald's and two strong coffees.

"Do me a favour," Swift said as they bumped over a small ford. "Get on the phone to Tink and ask her to dig into Grey Donovan. I want his life turned upside down and his pockets shaken out. We need as much info as we can get."

"Guv," Annie said, trying her best to fish out her phone without letting go of the handle.

"Oi," Swift said, giving her the side eye.

Annie rang Tink and relayed the information they had gathered from Peter Johnson without squealing at the corners too many times.

"I've got some interesting news too," Tink said, and Annie held the phone tighter to her ear. "Angels of the Water is strictly a local church group. They don't accept people outside of Norfolk, and to become a member of congregation you have to pay, which I think you already knew, but get this, you also have to be female."

"What!?" Annie said, repeating the new information to Swift. "But what about the leaders? Let me guess?"

"Yep," Tink replied. "All male."

"That's a pretty shitty way to prey on people at the best of times."

"Yep," Tink said again. "Right, I'll let you know when I've found any info on Grey Donovan. Safe travels, don't let Swift fool you into thinking he's a good driver."

"Oi," Swift bellowed across the car. "I heard that."

Annie dropped her phone in her lap. "What does that mean for these two lodgers then, if all of the congregation is female? That's so weird. It's making me dislike Richard Able and Peter Johnson even more than I already did."

"Yeah," Swift said, indicating right and turning into a new-build estate on the edge of a posh town that Annie knew had some great shops for those with pay packets that didn't come from the government. "I wonder if the church knows Peter is renting out his property to these men? We're nearly there, Annie. I don't know what we're going to find here but I'm not going to be upset or annoyed if you want to wait in the car for backup."

Adrenaline was coursing through Annie's veins faster than the thick espresso had done. "Not a chance, Swift, I'm coming in with you. Like you said, I'm part of your team now."

Swift momentarily took his eyes off the road and smiled at her. "Yes, you are!"

ANNIE COULD HEAR her own heartbeat so loudly that she feared it was about to send morse code to the men in the house and warn them that two detectives were about to descend on their hideout. Well, one detective and one psychotherapist masquerading as a detective. Either way, she was about to give their cover up. Swift had told her to stand behind him, so she was peering over his shoulder at the front door of a beige looking new-build in the middle of a street of other beige looking new-builds. Swift hammered at the door with his fists.

"Police!" he shouted. "Open up!"

There was no sound from inside the house. No movement through the glass in the front door. Swift bashed again and Annie moved away from him to try her luck at the window. The curtains to the front of the house were all drawn, despite the sun and the fact it was midday. She put her hands up against the glass to shield the glare and tried to peek in. It was useless; the curtains had been drawn together so tightly that there were no gaps. Sighing, she stepped back to Swift.

Swift tried the door handle. It didn't move. He lifted the flap of the letterbox. "Hello," he said through the gap. "It's the police, can you open up, please?"

As Swift moved back, Annie could just about make out an entrance hall through the gloom. But there was something else... an overwhelming stench coming through the letterbox.

"Can you smell that?" Annie whispered.

Swift nodded and stood back from the house, looking to either side and up to the first-floor windows. Annie knew he was looking for a way in, but the house was giving up none of its secrets.

"Excuse me?" A voice shouted over the fence.

Annie turned to see a woman with hair set so firmly it would probably stand up to a hurricane. She followed Swift as he trod down the weeds on the small patch of front garden to get to the neighbour.

"Are you the police?" the woman asked, and Annie heard Swift sigh.

"Yes we are," she replied, before Swift got there first and pissed the woman off. She looked like Mrs Bucket off the television, which made Annie's lips twitch at the corners. "Can you tell us when you last saw your neighbours?"

The woman craned her neck to see past Annie and Swift to the house beyond. Not that she'd see much if she managed.

"They're a quiet pair," she said, when she realised there was nothing to see. "Keep themselves to themselves. I did wonder, when the newer man moved in, if that would mean parties and the like. But so far there's been nary a peep. Except…"

She stopped talking, almost as though she was suddenly aware that it was the police she was talking to.

Swift stepped closer to the fence that separated them.

"Except what, Mrs…?" he asked, his face and voice neutral.

"Ms, I'm divorced. Ms Parker," she said, directing that line at Swift. "Except, oh you'll think I'm being silly."

"Of course we won't, Ms Parker," Swift said, smiling. Annie gave him credit where it was due. He knew when to turn on the charm. "Now, what were you were going to say? They were quiet except…"

Ms Parker shifted her weight and leant on the fence, conspiratorially.

"A few nights ago, I thought I heard crying."

Annie's skin started to crawl up her scalp and over her head. She saw a shift in Swift too.

"Crying?" he probed, his voice still calm.

"Yes," Ms Parker added, looking like she was enjoying this now. "It was weird, two grown men in there and the crying sounded like a woman, or… I don't know, possibly a child. It was keening, you know? But no one other than the two men went in or out."

She looked up from Swift to the sky as though it could tell her a story.

"Actually," she continued. "Truth be told, I wondered if they were, you know, *gay.*" She whispered the word as though it was a secret that didn't warrant sharing. "Are they in trouble?"

Swift pushed himself back from the fence, nodding at Annie to follow him.

"Thanks for your time, Ms Parker, you've been very helpful," he called over his shoulder as he walked back towards the house.

Annie could tell he was trying not to give away the urgency to get into the place, but his shoulders were taut, and his hands were balled into fists. Instead of hammering at the front door, Swift jumped the gate to the side passage, round to the back garden. Annie followed, glad she was wearing trainers. The back garden was as overgrown as the front and the grass came up to her knees, ripe with nettles.

The pair stood looking at the back of the house together. Its blank face impenetrable through closed curtains.

"Do you think they're in there?" Annie asked, her throat tight, her chest hammering.

"I don't know," Swift admitted. "But we need to get in there. Backup is too far away. Tell me, O'Malley. How do you feel about a little breaking and entering?"

"I'm all for it if it means saving some lives."

They were both over by the patio doors before Annie had finished her sentence. She looked around for a large rock, or a piece of garden furniture they could use to smash the double glazing. She'd heard a rumour that hitting new windows and doors in the corner would shatter the glass, and she hoped fervently that it wasn't just a rumour.

Swift spotted an old metal garden chair, upturned, hidden in the weeds. It could have been white, in its prime. Now it was a twisted corpse of rusty orange. He pulled his sleeves over his hands and picked it up.

Annie was about to move out of his way when she tugged the door handle just in case. To her surprise, the patio doors swung towards her, bringing with them a sweet, sickly stench she knew too well. She staggered backwards and Swift dropped the chair and was by her elbow in a second.

"Woah," he said, giving her a much-needed prop. "Everything alright?"

Annie nodded. "Yeah. Sorry. That smell…it just gets right in your pores."

Swift's face creased in disgust as he caught the whiff of sweat and faeces.

"Are you coming in?" he asked, his hand still holding her elbow. Annie pulled her T-shirt up over her mouth and nodded again.

They stepped into a dark, dank room that may in better circumstances have been a dining room. A table took up most of the space, its surface littered with blackened tin foil, straps of elastic, empty plastic bottles, dirty cups with layers of mould growing in them, and plates of food gone sour. The stench was chronic, like a sewer filling the room. Annie gagged.

"So much for rehab," Swift said, his voice muffled through his jumper. "This way."

They exited the room into a small hallway. Annie could see a filthy galley kitchen next to the dining room and a door opposite the stairs was shut.

"Hello!" Swift yelled the best he could through his makeshift mask. "It's the police. If there is anyone in the house, you need to make yourselves known."

They both stopped; Annie held her breath. But the house felt empty. Swift pulled a blue latex glove from his back pocket and over one hand, then turned the doorknob to the front room. It was like a different house. The carpet was still cream, two sofas were directed at the huge television, even the coffee table was free of stains. A single cup stood steaming in the middle.

Annie walked past Swift, looking down into the cup, and sniffing strong, good quality coffee. She could feel the heat of the drink on her face. As she straightened up, her stomach clenched in fear. Swift was staring at her, his latex-clad finger held to his lips. *Shhh.*

Annie froze. *What?*

Swift threw his eyes to the ceiling. A moment later, Annie heard a muffled thump. The pair ran to the stairs, and Swift threw himself up them two at a time, Annie not far behind him. Three closed doors faced them. Swift bashed open the first door he came to, an empty bathroom that was the hub of the stench trickling down to the rest of the house. The next door gave way to an immaculate bedroom, also empty except for a double divan bed. Annie's hand was trembling as she grabbed the handle of the last door and threw it open. Despite the dark enveloping the room, and the rotten meat stench permeating the air, Annie and Swift marched in, scanning from left to right. As her eyes became accustomed to the dimness, Annie could make out a figure, curled up in the corner, below the window. The small strip of light from under the closed curtains cut through the figure like a sparkler. Annie didn't dare breathe.

"Hello," Swift said, taking a step towards the motion-less figure. He reached out a gloved hand and bent forwards, fingers ready to find a pulse if necessary. "It's the police. Do you need assistance?"

As he reached the body, it rolled onto its side, and Annie felt bile fill her throat. The emaciated face of Tim Barclay stared at her through glassy eyes. Then he opened his mouth and let out a blood-chilling wail.

FOURTEEN

Friday

THE KNOCK AT HER OFFICE DOOR JOLTED ANNIE AWAKE. Unsure of what had rudely disturbed her, she peeled her eyes open, feeling as though she'd been hit by a bus that had then reversed back over her for good measure. Her head was thick with sleep, her mouth tasted like the rotten stench that had emanated throughout the house they'd broken into yesterday. *That house.* She took a swig from her water bottle and flipped over onto her back. It was as though she was waking after a night out clubbing. Back when she'd had a life and friends, and time and money to waste on £3 bottles of Smirnoff Ice or Blue WKD. The hangovers the next day had gradually gotten so bad that Annie had pretty much stopped drinking anything that was filled with artificial colours and flavours. Wine never left her feeling like this. But then again, alcohol hadn't done it at all this time.

A second loud rap at the door had Annie forgetting about sweet alcopops and darting for her clothes. She leapt out of the camp bed and dragged on sweats and a hoody, glancing at the clock on her desk as she did so.

10.15am, shit.

"Hang on, I'll be right there!" she shouted through the closed door as the knock came again.

Shit, shit, shit.

Annie's brain wasn't fuddled enough to forget clients. *Was it?* She ran a brush through her hair and chewed some toothpaste tabs from the little pot by the sink, hiding away the toiletries and personal paraphernalia as best she could. She opened the door, surprised to see Swift standing behind it.

"Everything alright?" Swift asked, looking around the office space as Annie let him in.

She glanced around, hoping that she'd hidden away enough of her stuff to fool him.

"Yeah, sorry, I was, um… you know."

Swift stared at Annie for long enough to make her cheeks flame.

"Sleeping?"

She turned away and headed for the kitchenette. "Top marks, Detective."

"I don't blame you," he said, taking a seat on one of the low comfy chairs she used for consultations. "I would be too, if I hadn't been woken by bloody foxes at it outside my bedroom window before it was even light."

Annie handed him a coffee. "It's just instant, hope that's okay?"

"Police station finest would be okay right now. I feel like the living dead."

"I *look* like the living dead."

Annie slid a window up and the sounds from the street below filtered in through their silence. Bicycle bells rang, delivery vans clattered, cars thudded over the cobbled road…people going about their normal lives. Annie wasn't sure, after the shock of what they'd found yesterday, what her normal life was anymore.

"How are you?" Swift asked, as he blew on the steaming cup in his hand.

Annie shrugged. *How am I?* "I honestly feel like I could sleep for a week and still not recover from the last few days. Is this, like, just an average day in the life of Joe Swift?"

Swift laughed, but there was no humour in it. "Thankfully, no."

"Good," Annie replied, sipping her coffee and starting to feel slightly more human with the fresh air and caffeine. "Because if I'm going to be consulting with you, I don't want to be feeling like this forevermore."

"You can step away from this if you need to, Annie," Swift said, looking concerned. "Like I said, *nothing* is worth losing your mind over."

"Two missing girls are," Annie said, pointedly.

Swift stared at her, shaking his head slowly. "Nothing."

The room was thick. Annie couldn't speak. She knew her personal need to find these girls was more than just finding these girls. Every time she thought about Jodie Carter or Orla Finch she pictured her little sister Mim, whisked away by their dad — ex-copper, pivotal member of society, until he wasn't. She couldn't get the cries out of her head; even though she hadn't been there when their dad had taken Mim, she knew how her sister sounded when she was upset. Crying for Mum over a grazed knee or a bumped head, or because her doll's hair had gotten too tangled. Those cries kept Annie awake at night, despite her efforts to forget.

"You're a psychotherapist, you of all people should know that you need to look after your own mental health."

Annie laughed. "I thought it was common knowledge that health professionals are the worst. We're all in denial, that's why it makes it so much easier to treat others."

"Touché," Swift said.

"So," Annie continued, finishing her coffee. "Tell me what we've got. How is Mr Barclay? Any news on Grey Donovan? That's why you're really here, isn't it?"

Swift's brow knotted. "You're good at that. Please don't delve too deep in here though." He tapped his temple.

"You've brought your work bag with you," Annie said, indicating the satchel Swift had dropped by his feet. "I've told you before, I can't read minds. I just read behaviour."

Swift smiled and reached for the bag. He drew out a file and opened it on his knee, resting his cup on top.

"Tim Barclay is in hospital," he began. "He's as okay as can be expected for someone who had heroin on tap for the last God knows how long. He's not going to be much use to us at the moment though, Tink went to see him last night and he's properly out for the count. The doctors will let us know when he's talking, but they're trying to keep us away so he can get better. His wife has been in to see him though. Maggie. It seems he'd not eaten properly for days, and was on the brink of death from lack of fluids. So much for charity, hey?"

"I doubt Peter Johnson ever visited his tenants."

"Likely not, he would have kicked them out if he'd seen the state of the house."

"Most of the house," Annie added, thinking about the

immaculate living room and how, what was most likely to be, Grey's bedroom had been almost untouched.

"Yeah," Swift agreed. 'That was weird."

"And Grey Donovan?" Annie asked.

"Grey Donovan is known to the police."

Annie nodded, unsurprised.

"Drugs?" she asked.

"No, weirdly enough." Swift flipped a sheet of paper in Annie's direction. "Solicitation. Lewd behaviour. Indecent assault."

Annie scanned the rap sheet handed to her. It was a photocopy, the handwriting difficult to decipher. It felt like something out of the nineties rather than up-to-date police files. The dates of the incidents all read at only a few years prior.

"Don't the custody suites in Norwich have twenty-first century equipment?" she asked, her eyes still scanning the long list.

"You're lucky we're not still using slate and chalk," Swift laughed. "Just because *probation* are allowed a computer each, don't get all conceited about it."

"Chance would be a fine thing," Annie said, her brows furrowing. "Did Donovan get charged with anything? It seems there's a lot of arrests and not much else."

Swift shook his head. "No, there was never enough evidence to get him on any of the charges, and witnesses and victims seemed to vanish into thin air at the crux."

"Bloody hell," Annie said, whistling through her teeth as she flipped the page over and stared at another load of assault arrests. "So have we brought him in for questioning then?"

"Nope," Swift said, slapping the file down onto the coffee table with a sting. "Our Mr Donovan has gone

AWOL. Hasn't been seen or heard from since last month, when the neighbour said she saw him."

"But there was a warm cup of coffee in the living room of that house that sure as hell wasn't Tim Barclay's," Annie said, exasperated. "That can't have been anyone other than Donovan, can it? *Shit.* Do you think Peter Johnson gave him the heads up?"

Swift nodded. "It's looking likely. We're bringing Johnson in for questioning as we speak. Checking his phone records too."

"And the paraphernalia, the house? Are we looking for, I don't know how it all works, DNA or something that will help us to track down the girls?"

Swift ran his hands through his hair, his attention drawn to the window and the noise of the streets below.

"The DCI isn't sure we're going to reach the threshold for CPS to issue us with a warrant to search the house," he said eventually.

"What?" Annie shouted. "But that's absurd. It's all connected to the church, surely? The dolls, the creepy symbols, the fact that Orla's dad was in a church property? The fact that the neighbour heard what she thought was a child crying. What more does your DCI need?"

"We can't arrest Tim Barclay on suspicion of kidnap, and there's not enough to connect Grey Donovan yet. We technically shouldn't have been in the property without a warrant, but we heard that cry from Barclay and had to help. The crying the neighbour heard, I think it was Tim's." Swift looked at her with steely eyes.

Annie knew damn well the cry they had heard came *after* they'd found Tim Barclay, but she wasn't going to argue with Swift when she agreed with everything they'd done. God knows how long Tim would have had left if they hadn't, in effect, broken the law and waltzed right on into a private property. Plus, Annie didn't fancy being arrested.

"Is that the other reason you're here? So we can get our story straight?" she asked.

"Story?" Swift asked, his mouth twisted into a smile of sorts.

"The way he cried out when we found him will stay with me for ever," Annie said, her shoulders shivering with the memory of Barclay's keening. "I'm happy to say we heard it from outside. And you're right, I was going to say that too. I think the neighbour heard Tim through the walls, he must have been in so much pain, the kind caused by, and only quashed by, a shit load of drugs."

"Yeah. We've seized the drugs and sent those for forensics. The baggies, the equipment, the stashes that Donovan had piled neatly in his bedroom. If there's anything of the girls on those items, we'll find out soon."

"Do we know where Donovan may have gone? Any friends or family around? What happened to his parents?" Annie asked.

"Tink is looking into that, along with the rest of his history. We need to get over to the station and get a round-up of new info. Plus, we need to go over what we found yesterday with the rest of the team."

"Sorry, I would have been there earlier, I must have slept through my alarm," Annie said, feeling like she'd failed her first week back at police work only four days in.

"Don't apologise, O'Malley," Swift said, his eyes coming back to her.

"Right, sorry," Annie said, before realising what she'd said and laughing.

"Do you want a lift to the station?" Swift said, hauling himself out of the low chair.

"No, I'm good," Annie replied, taking their cups to the kitchenette and swirling cold water around them. "I think I'm going to walk over. I feel like the fresh air will do me some favours this morning."

"Fair enough," he said, grabbing his bag.

Annie opened the door for him and stood leaning against it, watching Swift throw his bag on his shoulder and move towards her. He was so sure of himself, even though he took up a lot of space. She liked that about him.

"So," Swift said as he stepped out into the stairwell. "When were you going to tell me you were living *in* your office and not above it?"

Annie grimaced and swung the door shut in his face.

FIFTEEN

"OKAY TEAM," SWIFT SAID, BASHING HIS CUP DOWN ON the desk so hard that the coffee splashed over the side and onto the Formica. He wiped it away with the sleeve of his jumper. "Let's summarise where we're at."

Annie looked up from her computer and hit the button to send the screen to sleep. She'd been doing a bit of digging but didn't want any roving eyes to judge her, she still felt out of her depth and was pretty sure she'd be arrested for fraud if they saw she was Googling answers to her million and one questions. She had enjoyed the walk from her flat-come-office to the station though. The late summer sun was still warm, and the city had been full of shoppers and walkers and people who generally looked happy to be there. Her mind had been racing through the details that Swift had woken her with. The rap sheet, the drugs, the fact that their DCI didn't think there was enough evidence to get a search warrant for the property. Her blood had started to boil as she'd arrived at the crowd of protestors gathered for today's vigil outside the station. Cursing herself for forgetting to go around to the back doors, she'd pushed her way through the throng that was chanting *stop the cuts* and *save our services*. Under her breath, she'd joined in.

Rose had waved her through the front doors with a smile.

"Oi, you," she'd hissed to Annie in the empty lobby. "What's going on with you and Swift?"

Annie had felt her cheeks heat and she had whisked herself over to Rose with her forefinger up to her lips. "Shhhh," she'd said. "That's how rumours start."

"So?" Rose had shrugged, her eyes sparkling. "This station could do with a good rumour or two. It's been dull as anything since those protestors took up residence. People who would pop in to report something menial, like old Mrs Smith who used to come in at least once a week to moan about the bin men smiling at her suspiciously, they've all but dried up. They don't like having to squeeze past the protestors."

"Shouldn't the police officers here just *move them on*?" Annie had asked, leaning an arm on the reception desk. "Isn't that a thing they can do?"

Rose had shrugged again. "I guess they like the lack of paperwork that comes with the relative quiet."

Then she'd slapped both hands down on the desk. "But stop digressing. Tell me all about why you and Swift turned up together first thing in the morning looking like you'd had no sleep?"

Annie had been about to, but the inner doors had slid open with a hiss and Swift himself beckoned Annie over.

"Sorry," Annie had smiled at Rose, who looked apoplectic. "Work to be doing." She'd blown her a kiss and headed into the inner sanctum of the station.

.   .   .

"OKAY, PAGE, TALK TO ME," Swift said, heading over to the noticeboard and poking a finger at the picture of Jodie Carter. "What did you find out about Jodie's dad?"

The younger detective picked a sheet of paper from his desk and walked to the front of the room, where Swift was standing next to the noticeboard.

"Okay," Page said, tacking the sheet to the board next to Jodie's young face. "The possible paternity of Jodie Carter was narrowed down to two men when we pushed Tammy Carter for information."

"She was feeling a bit off-colour, Guv," he added. "So getting the information out of her took a lot longer than it needed. She kept having to excuse herself. I hope it was nothing contagious."

Swift grimaced. "I hope you washed your hands thoroughly and changed clothes once you were done? The last thing we need is a bout of a bloody sickness bug."

Page grimaced in a way that told Annie he had probably come straight back to the station after his interview.

"Anyway," Page said, moving the conversation away from his possible contamination of the whole team. "Tammy Carter was actually quite forthcoming with information when she was feeling well. The Family Liaison Officer with her has been great. I think Tammy may have been a bit off with you guys on Tuesday because she's had a bad experience in the past."

"With the police?" Annie asked.

"Yeah," Page shook his head. "Mainly to do with the people she used to hang around with, back when she was pregnant with Jodie, apparently. Nothing came of it, she was too worried about her baby to stay involved. Anyway, the FLO has brought her round to see us as her friends now, and she wants to do anything she can to get Jodie back. I really felt for her."

"Back to the paternity," Swift barked and Page flinched.

"Yes, sorry. Tammy had two lovers at the time she fell pregnant. A…" Page stopped to consult the sheet of paper he'd just pinned to the board. "Lyle Baxter and a Brad Greene."

"Sorry," Annie said, sitting up straighter in her chair. "Did you say Lyle Baxter?"

Page nodded, looking cautiously at Swift. "Yes, local guy. Been in prison for affray and possession."

"Got out at the beginning of the year, yes I know," Annie said. "He was one of mine. Hold on."

Annie flicked her screen back on and clicked on the intranet icon. She logged into her work emails and scrolled down to the emails from January.

"Yes," she said, pointing at the screen though no-one could see it. "Here. Lyle Baxter. He's only twenty-two, was given a two-year sentence because it wasn't his first offence. Went down three years ago, so Jodie would have been just over a year. From what I can remember — and it's going back over six months now, and I can barely remember what I had for breakfast — Lyle had no idea he was a father. Or he was a very good liar."

"Do you often ask your clients if they're fathers?" Swift asked.

"Not routinely, no," Annie raised an eyebrow. "But we talk about things that are important and if there are children involved, then almost one hundred percent of the time they're brought up in conversation."

"Right," Swift conceded, and Annie tried to remain poker-faced

"That would make sense," Page continued. "Tammy Carter said she had never told either of the men about Jodie."

"But if he didn't know then surely he can't be a suspect?" Annie asked.

Page bounced his head from shoulder to shoulder. "It depends. If he's only just found out then maybe he wanted to get to Jodie, get revenge on Tammy for keeping her out of his life?"

"But then why take Orla too? And why leave a bloody corn doll in their place?" Annie asked, her turn to be exasperated.

"Let's get this Lyle Baxter in for questioning," Swift barked. "He may not know he's a father, but he can give us information on Tammy Carter and her associates. We can also find out if he knew Tim Barclay. If it slips that he's a dad, then so be it. Let's try and speak to the other guy too, whatsisname again?"

"Brad Greene?" Page nodded, though Annie could see hesitation on his face.

"Anything else?" Swift asked.

Page shook his head this time and retreated to his desk.

"Tink?" Swift asked, scanning the room for DS Lock.

"Yup," Tink said, bouncing to her feet and chicaning the desks to the front of the room. "Okay, so as I told Annie and Guv earlier, the Angels of the Water have a weird, archaic rule that only men can be leaders and that all their congregation have to be female."

Page snorted loudly.

"Yeah, I know. But apart from their set-up being totally middle ages, there's nothing to suggest that this would make them likely to abduct two young females. My work on this is still ongoing though."

"O'Malley?" Swift nodded at her.

Annie's stomach shrank at the thought of speaking in front of the team. But she wasn't going to let a little imposter syndrome and borderline glossophobia beat her.

"The symbols we found in Orla's bedroom, the trinity knot and the encircled five star," Annie said, half up out of her seat, not knowing if she should stand at the front like everyone else. "I've just been doing some more research on what they mean. They're the symbols of an all-powerful being and the devil, respectively. They're originally pagan. What affiliation are The Angels, if any? Are they similar in beliefs; any signs of paganism or the occult? Are they a church with new-age beliefs? Or is that just a cover-up for their sexist misogyny?"

Tink smiled at Annie and she felt encouraged.

"I looked at all their paperwork," Tink said. "Flyers, notepads, stationery etc, and there were no symbols anywhere on them. Except the Angels of the Water logo." Tink pointed to a printout tacked to the noticeboard depicting the logo that Annie recognised from the flyer she'd found in Maggie Finch's house.

It had an ink outline, teal blue on white, with three singular wavy lines depicting the sea rolling along the bottom. The naked, busty outline of a woman rose from the water, her arms raised to the heavens, wings spreading out to the edges of the paper. The wings, alone, were coloured in, the same teal as the line drawing. It certainly made an impact.

"Okay, thanks Tink," Annie said, dropping back into her seat. "There's something linking the church and the two girls, I can feel it."

Swift nodded slowly. "I think you're right. What aren't

we seeing?" He looked at the board and the ever-increasing papers tacked to the blue fabric.

"Apart from what I told you yesterday," Tink added. "There's no new stuff on Grey Donovan yet. There's been no sightings and he's not given himself up. We're waiting on forensics from Barclay's clothes."

"Get them to hurry it up," Swift said, rubbing his face in his hands before turning to the rest of the room. "Thanks guys. Right Annie!"

His barking her name made Annie jump.

"Yes, Guv?"

"Do you want to tell the guys what we found yesterday?"

Annie nodded and stood back up again. Upright this time, with gusto.

"As you know, Swift and I went to pay a visit to the North Norfolk church leader Peter Johnson," she began. She talked the team through the interview and the revelation about Tim Barclay that Johnson had hit them with right at the end. She then described the house owned by the church and what they'd found inside. The incongruous rooms, the smell of decay and faeces, the drugs, the half dead father of Orla Finch. But no sign of the missing girls.

As Annie was coming to the end of her story, the phone rang, shrill across the now quiet room. Tink slunk away to pick it up and eyes returned to Annie.

"And that," she finished. "Is pretty much it."

Page gave a wince. "Can we bring Johnson in on anything, if he called Grey Donovan to warn him you were on the way?"

Annie looked to Swift for the answer to that one.

"Neither Donovan nor Johnson have technically done anything illegal. So no."

"Obstruction?" Page asked.

"Possibly," Swift conceded, with a shrug. "Maybe possession if he knew about the drugs?"

"Why else would he call to warn Donovan?" Annie asked.

"That," Swift said pointedly. "Is the million-dollar question. Was it just because of the drugs, or was there something else? Donovan didn't exactly take his time to clear the drugs away. Which makes me think it's the latter."

"Let's get Johnson in on obstruction, then. And get his phone records checked. He will probably cry for a solicitor, but we'll make him stew for a bit first. Page, get a call out to patrol to go and bring him in. Annie, you and I are going to find out the hierarchy of this bloody church and head right to the top."

"No need to radio patrol, Guv," Tink shouted from across the room, slamming the phone down. "It's Peter Johnson. He's waiting for you in reception."

SIXTEEN

Peter Johnson's swagger had deserted him somewhere between the North Norfolk coast and the city police station. He looked a shell of the man Annie had faced up to yesterday. His suit jacket dwarfed him and his trainers were incongruous with the rest of his outfit. Even his stubble looked unruly. Annie eyed him through the glass doors as he sat with his head in his hands on one of the plastic seats in reception.

Swift had told her to go and bring him through. He thought that a little bit of antagonism would wind him up enough to spill his secrets in anger. And they could both tell from their last meeting that Peter Johnson hated women, especially women in power.

Annie straightened her jumper and ran her fingers through her hair to try and give it a bit of life. It felt as flat as she did. Who knew hair could be exhausted? Throwing her shoulders back she slid the doors open and strode across the reception.

"Mr Johnson?" she said, her voice booming. "Come with me, please."

Peter Johnson looked up at her, the dark circles beneath his eyes more prominent up close. He dragged himself to his feet; seemingly he'd shrunk a few inches since yesterday too. She wondered what was pulling him down as she led him through the sliding doors with a flick of Swift's pass on the keypad.

"Wait here, please," she said, opening the door to an interview room. "Can I get you a tea or a coffee?"

"Coffee please, black, no sugar." He took the plastic chair at the table, his body slouching into the curves.

Annie remembered the coffee machine and the espresso Peter Johnson had offered them and made a note to get his coffee from the vending machine.

"WHAT CAN you tell us about Grey Donovan?" Swift asked, his voice travelling across the interview room as he shut the door and took a seat opposite Peter Johnson.

Annie took the seat next to Swift and passed a watery black coffee in a thin plastic cup over the table. Peter Johnson's face dropped when he saw it but, to his credit, he kept his mouth shut and took it without complaint.

"I knew he was still doing drugs," Johnson said, collapsing. His head fell forwards onto his hands, propped up by elbows that looked too shaky to support them. "But I didn't know he had so much gear on him in my house. Honest."

"You're looking at a pretty harsh sentence if you're found guilty of possession with intent to sell, Johnson," Swift said, and Johnson's eyes widened in horror.

"I came here today of my own accord. I'm not under arrest, am I?" he whimpered. "I'd lose my job and my house, and my church leadership. I honestly had no idea. I thought he was just doing the odd spiff or whatever."

"Sp/iff?" Annie corrected. "You thought it was just weed he was using?"

"Spiff, spliff, whatever," Johnson said, shaking his head so much that Annie thought he'd give himself whiplash. "I knew he used to use hard drugs, but they said he'd stopped that. That he just smoked now. I thought they meant cigarettes. I don't know. I have never even touched the stuff. He doesn't come across like someone who uses all the time. He goes out, he has a life. I wish I'd never rented him the place, my other tenants have all been great."

"Did the church normally find your tenants?" Annie asked, picking up on what Johnson had just said. "Or do you do it yourself?"

Johnson wiped his eyes with the back of his hand.

"Myself, normally?" he said, his eyes now darting between Annie and Swift. "But sometimes we're asked by the council, as they have a duty of care to help house people in private accommodation when they can't provide social housing. But the order to house Grey came from right at the top. I couldn't say no. But he never told me he was dealing to Tim Barclay, or what a state Mr Barclay was in. Is he going to be okay?"

"Why did you warn Grey Donovan we were on the way to the house?" Swift asked, ignoring the question. "What else did he have there that you needed him to get rid of? Why did he leave and not take anything incriminating with him? Or maybe he did take something with him. Two things. We're investigating the abduction of two four-year old girls here, Mr Johnson. I suggest you give us some answers."

"Surely you don't think I had anything to do with that?" Johnson sat up in his chair now, his face like a rabbit cornered by a whippet. "This is drugs. Just drugs. Nothing else. I couldn't take young girls away from their families. Why would I? What would I want with two young girls? Please? You have to believe me. I didn't know this was going to happen. I thought… I just. Please? This has nothing to do with those girls."

"Tim Barclay is the dad of Orla Finch, one of the missing girls. Don't you watch the news?"

The whites of Peter Johnson's eyes were bulging in their sockets. "What? No. No. I had been told that the police were looking for Tim, but I had no idea why."

"Who told you that?" Swift barked.

"Donovan," Johnson sobbed. "He told me they'd lay low for a bit. I thought it was the drugs. Nothing else. Oh bloody hell. What should I do?"

Annie was almost starting to feel sorry for Peter Johnson. Almost.

"Tell us why you called Grey Donovan to give him the heads up that we were on our way," she said.

Tears ran down Johnson's face and he made a futile attempt to wipe them away with his jacket sleeve. But it just spread them further.

"I thought he needed to move Tim out of the house for a bit. Even though I'd told you he was there. If you couldn't find him immediately, there was a chance he could get rid of some of the drugs before you did find him. I thought I was helping him. Helping them both. I need the income from the house. And the church told me I needed to look out for him"

"Thanks for coming in today, Mr Johnson," Swift said, standing abruptly. "We'll be in touch if we need any more information. And don't leave the country, will you?"

Annie and Swift left the interview room. Swift barked orders at the PC manning the door to show Mr Johnson out of the station.

"Grab your coat, Annie," he said. "We're going to find the head of this bloody church and work out what's *actually* going on."

SEEMINGLY, the funds for the Angels of the Water didn't trickle down to its followers, rather it was shoved upwards in vast quantities. The house of Amadeus Hyde, the registered company director of the church, was at the end of a driveway longer than Annie's entire street. It circled around in front of the building, enclosing a fountain that trickled with fresh, clear water. The building itself looked like it had been plucked from the National Trust brochure. Annie yanked the bell pull and they stood back as the ringing sounded out past the thick wooden door and the gothic Victorian red brick.

"I wondered when you'd get here." Amadeus was a small man who reminded Annie of a mouse. He pulled the door back to reveal marble floors so clean they dazzled. "Please remove your shoes and use the hand gel supplied."

Annie looked around. There was no furniture in the echoey hallway. Just glistening bannisters and polished doors, and the abrasive smell of bleach. Amadeus wore a smoking jacket that made him look like Hugh Hefner and white cotton gloves that made him look like he belonged on a psychiatric ward. He stood right back, not getting within three feet of either Annie or Swift as they slipped out of their shoes, or kicked them off in Swift's case, and pumped the sticky gel onto their hands. The strong smell made Annie wince. Amadeus led them through to a room straight off the hallway, much to Annie's dismay — she had been hoping for more of a tour. The room was as sparse as the hallway had been. Three white sofas were placed around a white rug, and a small side table held yet more hand gel. The hairs on Annie's neck were already standing to attention.

"Please take a seat." Amadeus stayed standing, carefully inspecting each sofa first but obviously finding something untoward that stopped him sitting down himself. "Now officers, tell me how I can help."

His syrupy voice sent chills down Annie's back. She glanced sideways at Swift, who also seemed to be out of his depth. A look she'd not seen on him before.

"Can you tell us what you know about Peter Johnson?" she asked, feeling okay about making the first move.

"He's been an Angel leader since our conception. Coming up to ten years ago now. We have a large celebration planned with our congregation this weekend."

He spoke in clipped sentences that made Annie feel seasick.

"And did you know that Peter Johnson was renting his house out to a drug dealer?" Swift asked, still standing, his hand rubbing confrontationally on the back of one of the sofas.

"Do you have any proof that the man living there was dealing the drugs?" Amadeus asked, unperturbed.

"Why else have thousands of pounds worth of gear if you're not going to flog it?"

"Why indeed," Amadeus answered. "But that in itself?

Not proof. There is nothing. Nothing to tie the church to this. Our leaders are individuals. Perfectly capable of their own actions."

"Why did you want Grey housed in Peter Johnson's house?" Swift continued.

"Would you not want to help a young man in need?"

"What can you tell us about Richard Able?" Annie asked, when Amadeus didn't get a reply to his question.

A shiver ran through Amadeus's whole body at the mention of the man's name.

"Mr Able is…" Amadeus started, wiping an invisible speck of dust from his immaculate shoulder. "Somewhat unorthodox."

Pot and kettle, thought Annie. The height of Swift's eyebrows indicated that he shared her thought.

"In what way?" she asked.

"The way he lives," Amadeus answered.

"Not in the way he conducts his church business?" Swift interrupted.

"He is free to tend to his congregation the best way he sees fit." Amadeus said, his voice level. "Like I just said. Our leaders are their own person."

"And what can you tell us about Orla Finch or Jodie Carter?" Swift asked, running his hands along the back of the sofa, Amadeus's eyes following the movement with a rising panic.

"I'm sorry, who?" he asked, regaining his composure.

"The missing girls," Annie replied, taking a step towards Amadeus. "Surely you've seen the news? One of the girls lives near Richard Able, the other happens to live near Peter Johnson."

"Coincidence, I'm sure." Amadeus seemed nonplussed at the mention of the missing girls. But he seemed nonplussed at most of the conversation. The only thing getting the slightest change in emotion was the noise of Swift's hand as it glided across the back of the white material.

"We have reason to believe that the church is somehow connected to the abductions, and we will do everything in our power to find those girls," Swift said, wiping his face with his hand before putting it back on the sofa. "Even if that means coming back here with a warrant to search these premises thoroughly. And we're not tidy about it."

Swift had had enough, he moved towards the door. Annie started to follow him but the sound of Amadeus laughing had her rooted to the spot. The cold, calculated gurgles chilled her right through.

"I'm sorry," she said, her brow furrowed, her heart pounding. "Is there something funny about two abducted toddlers?"

Amadeus finished laughing before he spoke. The very act a show of how much power he felt he held.

"You have me wrong," he said, his dead eyes burrowing into Annie's. "I'm not laughing at the girls. I'm laughing at your colleague's arrogance. I'll see you out."

"We'll see ourselves out," Annie said, following Swift out the door and slipping her shoes on as quickly as she could.

Something was very wrong in this house. Annie needed some fresh air and she desperately wanted to go home and have a nap. She was feeling totally exhausted as she dragged the front door towards her and stepped into the heat of the sun.

Swift was right behind her, his phone beeping in his

hand. He shook his head and took some deep breaths before glancing down at the screen.

"Tim Barclay is awake," he said, looking up at Annie, and she shelved the idea of rest for another day.

SEVENTEEN

ANNIE CREPT THROUGH THE DOOR OF TIM'S ROOM. THE sounds of the machines littering the place were loud and incessant, Annie had no idea how he could sleep through the beeps and whirs. But sleep he did. The charge nurse had given Swift and Annie the run-down of how Tim had been awake for a couple of hours earlier, but his demeanour had been withdrawn and he'd barely spoken to anyone. As he'd already fallen back to sleep by the time they got there, Annie had offered to wait for him to wake again. Swift had gone to clear the bleach out of his nostrils with police station coffee and find out how far along forensics were with the clothes and drugs from the house of horror.

Lines of painkillers, antibiotics, and fluids ran from the three bags above Tim's bed to the cannula in the back of his wrist. Wrapped up in his standard issue, NHS blue waffle blanket, Tim looked a lot older than his twenty-five years. Annie pulled over a chair and sank into the wipeable cushions. She had started to nod off when Tim's voice woke her from her daydream.

"Miss O'Malley?" he croaked, shuffling upright onto his elbows.

His face was gaunt; his cheeks caved and his teeth prominent. Annie tried not to stare. He looked like he was still on the brink of starvation. Bandages hid the track marks up his arms, but nothing could hide the fear in his eyes.

"Wait a minute," Annie said, hunting for the remote for the bed and lifting its head so Tim could take the weight off arms that looked like they might snap at any second. "There, is that better?"

Tim nodded. "What are you doing here, Miss O'Malley? Am I in trouble for missing my last session? I never meant to. It all happened so quickly, I just forgot to come and see you."

Annie had almost forgotten the working relationship she'd had with Tim in the previous weeks, so much had happened in the last few days. But he was the reason she was on this case, and she owed him the truth. She thought it was strange that he hadn't mentioned Orla yet, though. Surely the first thought of a parent on waking would be about their child? Annie didn't know for sure, as she had none of her own, but Tim's daughter was missing, and asking about her should be a given. Either he knew she was safe, or he had no idea she was missing.

"I'm not here to tell you off for missing a session, Tim," she said, gently. "I need to talk to you about Orla."

Tim looked down; a flush rose up behind the layer of grey.

"I feel awful. For Orla and for Maggie. I never meant to hurt them."

"What do you mean by that, Tim?"

He looked back up at Annie, his eyes filled with tears.

Her heart raced, was he about to confess to hurting his daughter?

"I was off the drugs," he started, pausing for a moment to take a sip of the water. "I promise. I hadn't really done any since I got out of prison. But…"

He stopped again.

Annie kept quiet. She knew, after years of counselling work, that most people with something to say would fill any silence. The machines continued their constant noise and Annie could feel a trickle of sweat making its way down her spine towards the waistband of her trousers. No matter what the season, hospitals were always a few degrees too hot for Annie. Bloody patients and their need to stay warm. She took the time to stare out of the window behind Tim's bed. The sky was so blue, it looked right out of a children's cartoon. Not a cloud to sully it.

After a while it became clear that Tim had no desire to fill the gap left by Annie's questions, so she probed further. "But what, Tim?"

He jolted at her voice, and she realised he had simply nodded off again. She felt bad. "Sorry, Tim. I didn't mean to startle you. It's just really important that we talk to you right now."

Tim's face creased with worry. "Why? Has something happened to Grey?"

"What can you tell me about Grey?" Annie dodged the question like a pro.

"He," Tim bit his lip. "I don't want him to get in trouble. He's just a guy like me."

"Trust me, Tim," Annie said, with a growing sense of unease that Tim had no idea about Orla. "Drug trouble is the least of our worries right now. I'm not making any promises but if it's just drugs then I'll do my best to keep Grey out of trouble."

It didn't count if you crossed your fingers when you said it, did it? Not when there were missing children at stake.

"I was off the drugs," Tim continued, still wary. "You saw me. You know I was. I was doing really well and then I bumped into Grey at the local. I'd never seen him there before. He said he was new to the area and had just moved in, was looking for some friends. I'd been in that position myself, and I thought *what's the harm?*" He laughed ironically. "Stupid. *Stupid.* We had a lot in common. Age and that. Grey loves a bet on the dogs too. We hit it off. It was nice having a guy to hang out with. But then he started smoking weed when we were at his house. And that soon turned to a line of coke or a pill."

Tim looked down at his bandaged arm, his brows heavy.

"I'm not that strong. He was offering me smack. And I was injecting before you could say addict. I hated myself for it. I still do. I let down everyone who was there for me. Including you, Miss O'Malley."

"Is that why you moved out?"

Tim nodded. "I had to. I couldn't put Maggie through that again. And I couldn't risk putting Orla in that position. How are they? Do they hate me? I can't say I blame them. I'm so weak. If only I could have said no. But free drugs, man. You can't turn that shit down."

Annie took Tim's hand in hers. His skin felt paper soft, as though he wasn't there at all.

"Tim," she said, wishing there was a FLO or an actual police officer here to help her. "I'm sorry to be the one to break this to you, but the reason we needed to talk to you so urgently was to do with Orla. She's missing."

What was left of the blood in Tim's face soon drained away. His face caved in on its bones, as hollow as Annie felt right then.

"What?" he whispered. "Is it my fault? Did she run away?"

Annie shook her head. "It looks as though she was taken. Can you tell me, do you have any association with the Angels of the Water, apart from living in their house? Do you know anything about the meaning of a corn doll?"

"Taken?" Tim's eyes were like saucers. "What do you mean *taken*? And what do you mean about the house? I thought it was Grey's house, like he rented it and everything. You think Grey is the one who took Orla? I'll fucking kill him. Let me out of here, I'll fucking kill him."

Tim struggled with the blue blanket wrapped tightly around his legs. The machines were all working overtime now, their beeping had stepped up a notch.

"No," Annie said, her hand still on his, but she couldn't hold him for much longer. "No, we don't know who has Orla. It's just a line of enquiry, that's all."

Her lines sounded fake and glib now. She wasn't a police officer, she'd left all that behind her years ago. She shouldn't be the one telling Tim this.

Damn you, Swift.

A nurse came crashing through the door and shot Annie a look of pure disgust.

"What's going on here?" she said, leaning over Tim and checking his pulse against her fob watch. "Tim, love, you need to calm down."

Tim was thrashing away at the wires in his chest now, trying and failing to pull them free.

"I need to get out of here, my daughter is missing. I'll kill him!" he spat, his body getting weaker as the nurse rolled her fingers over one of the wheels on his drip stand. "I'll... kill... him."

"I think you need to leave, young lady." The nurse wasn't asking.

Tim fell back on the bed into a deep sleep. There wasn't much else for Annie to find out here. She'd done enough. Quite literally.

Annie's office felt cold despite the sun streaming through the large sash windows at the front. She closed the door and turned the lock. Maybe it wasn't the place that felt cold, maybe it was the lack of sleep, rest, and hot food that was the problem. She filled the kettle and threw the switch. Then double backed on herself and headed back down the stairs.

"Annie!" Pete the chef cried as she walked into the pizzeria. "Where have you been?"

He got a little closer and pulled out the chair at her favourite table. "Where *have* you been?" He looked at her quizzically. "You look like shite!"

"New work role," she said by means of explanation. "Can I have the usual and a large glass of red, please?"

Pete nodded slowly, his head swaying as he took in Annie's exhausted features.

"What are they making you do? Wrestle alligators?"

Annie huffed out an ironic laugh. "Worse, Pete! You don't want to know."

He threw his tea towel over his shoulder and started back for the kitchen. "You wouldn't catch me being run into the ground by the local government," he said over his shoulder.

Annie laughed properly then. Pete was always run off his feet making the world's best pizza, and he was always complaining about it. But, she supposed, it wasn't the government ordering the pizzas, not unless she counted herself. Pete dropped her wine off, and Annie took a large sip, savouring the soft warm feeling as it slid down into her stomach. Almost immediately she felt her shoulders drop from where they'd been hanging out making friends with her ears for the last few days.

"That bad, huh?" Pete asked as he dropped her pizza on the table in front of her and drizzled it generously with garlic oil.

"It's just something I've been asked to help with. I can't say no. But it's left me feeling a bit drained, that's all," she smiled weakly at him.

"Tough," he said, setting down the oil and grinding the pepper until the pizza was covered in a liberal sprinkling. "Do you want to talk about it?"

"Thanks, Pete," she said, looking up at him. "I can't though. Client confidentiality and all that. Well, actually, it's police confidentiality this time."

"Police?"

"Yeah," Annie said, slicing through her pizza with the cutter and then lifting a piping hot slice to her lips. "I'm working on the missing girls case."

"The two who have been abducted?" Pete's eyes widened. "I saw it on the news earlier, they were talking about a possible connection with that weird church?"

"That's the one."

"Well, no wonder you look so pooped," he said, pulling the chair out opposite Annie and taking a seat.

Annie sighed inwardly. The last thing she felt like doing was talking about how they were getting nowhere with any of the leads, or how she practically scared one of the parents to death that afternoon with her lack of tact. Not that she could talk about it anyway.

"I did some work with the Angels once," Pete said, tapping the side of his nose with his forefinger. "Catering. They love a good pizza and who am I to argue if they think I'm the best of the best? There was something weird about the lot of them if you ask me. A load of men sitting around talking about how they're going to take over the coastal villages, rule the big cities, and have the women eating out of the palms of their hands. It takes a wrong sort to want to have that much control over people."

"When was this, Pete?" Annie asked, her interest piqued, her pizza momentarily forgotten in her hand.

"Four or five months ago," he said, taking a slice of pizza for himself and tucking in. "They were at their annual general meeting from the sounds of it. And they've asked me to cater for their church birthday party this weekend too."

"Have they now?"

"Have you been there? To their headquarters?"

Annie nodded. "Amadeus Hyde's house? It's not what I imagined. He's a bit of a clean freak, isn't he?"

Pete shook his head. "No, not his house. The actual headquarters? The old, converted barn in Flynt? It's like some sort of shrine to pagan gods, all candles here and weird symbols etched into the floor there. I'm not sure I want to go there again, but they're paying triple the cost price, so I can't afford to turn it down."

"Wait," Annie shouted. "Backtrack a little. Did you say there are candles and weird symbols there?"

Pete nodded, picking up another slice of Annie's pizza.

"I'm sorry, Pete," Annie cried. "I've got to go. Text me the address of the barn, would you? And I'll pay for all this next time I'm in. Though you can go halves seeing as you're the one eating it!"

She grabbed a slice and ran out the door, her phone already connecting to Swift's.

EIGHTEEN

THE BARN LOOKED AS THOUGH IT HAD SEEN BETTER DAYS. Swift flicked his torch on just as Annie turned off the car headlights, sending the barn into an eerie darkness for a split second. All thoughts of an early night had flown out of the window when Pete had mentioned this place. Something in Annie's waters had shifted and she knew they had to check it out, though she wished she'd *actually* shifted her waters before jumping in the car and picking Swift up. All the way to the coast she'd been dying for the loo, and it wasn't like she could squat behind a tree now, as the barn was smack bang in the middle of a corn field with no trees in sight.

Swift swept the torch beam back and forth, taking in the crumbling brick building with its moss-green pitched roof. It was larger than Annie had expected. And older. Given how modern the church houses were, she had been expecting some new-fangled barn conversion with glass frontage and trees shaped like spheres in pots at the door. As it was, the only things standing sentry at the rickety-looking doors were two great masses of stinging nettles.

Why is this place so hidden and derelict?

Annie took out her phone and hit the torch symbol, the hairs standing to attention on the back of her neck. She followed the beam to the small dusty window at the side of the barn and peered in. There was no way of seeing through the darkness, and the light just bounced off the filthy glass, making it hard to see anything other than the spots of white that were now etched onto her eyeballs.

"Here try this," Swift said, heading over to the door and rattling the padlock, held on by a thick chain wrapped around the door handles. "Hmm. How can we break and enter this one without getting into trouble?"

Annie pushed at the window, but it didn't budge, probably held shut with years of grime. She joined Swift at the door.

"Maybe there's a loose panel somewhere," she said, looking to the corner of the barn. "It's not in the best condition."

"Maybe," Swift replied, before sending a kick to the door that looked most likely to give way. The door buckled under the strain and fell off its bottom hinge, hanging like a loose tooth from the frame. "Bloody kids, they're such vandals."

He bent down and lifted the door at an angle so Annie could climb through into the space. She held up her phone torch, trying not to show Swift just how much her hands were shaking.

The inside was a totally different kettle of fish to the outside.

Annie swept her torch around, taking in the creepy interior, when the whole place suddenly lit up like the Blackpool Illuminations.

"What the—" she spun around and saw Swift smiling beside a light switch covered in a thick grey plastic casing.

"Et voila," he said, mimicking the stance of a magician who had just made a woman disappear.

Annie's skin crawled. The exterior of the barn was obviously a ruse to keep people out. The inside was clean and dry, and looked like it had been used very recently. Annie thought back to what Pete had said about it giving him the creeps and she could see why. Chairs were set out in a perfect circle around the edge of the main room. At the centre of the circle, carved into the floor in crude lines, was the Angels of the Water symbol. The walls of the barn were dotted with candle holders, their candles melted almost to the wicks, while in between the metal sconces were symbols created in thick red paint. At least, Annie hoped it was paint. She didn't recognise any of the symbols as those drawn on Orla's window, but they could have been from the same book of the occult.

She walked further into the large space, urging her feet to keep moving despite her brain screaming at her to turn and run away. Swift wasn't far behind her; she could hear his footsteps on the wooden floor. The room felt warm, not as she imagined. It was as though someone had only just turned off the electric heater that was standing out like a sore thumb at the back of the room.

Maybe they had.

The thought occurred to her that maybe they weren't alone. Holding her breath, she stepped up to the heater and placed the back of her hand against it. It was cold to the touch. Annie let out the breath and turned to Swift.

"It's the wood," he said, before she could speak. "It stores the heat from the sun and keeps hold of it."

He walked up to join her. "I remember going to

Sunday school in a wooden church hut, like, a normal one, not this satanic weirdness, and during the summer months we'd be baking in our own juices by the end of the Lord's Prayer."

"*You* went to Sunday school?" Annie laughed, relief flooding her body that they were alone in this creepy place.

"I'll have you know I was a pillar of the community back then," he winked. "Still am."

"When you're not kicking in doors and entering premises without a warrant!" Annie laughed again.

"Needs must," he shrugged. "Have you seen any symbols that may link in with our missing kids?"

Annie shook her head, walking up to the nearest symbol splashed onto the wood, a large eye with a scythe in the middle of the pupil. She lifted a finger to touch the paint as it bubbled out in thick brush strokes. It was cool to touch too, and dry.

"What do you think they're doing here?" she asked. Annie had told Swift about the annual general meeting that Pete and his pizzas had attended on the drive out to the coast. But this felt nothing like any conference room that Annie had ever been in. "Why use this when they have all those houses, or even Amadeus's house?"

Swift shook his head, "Amadeus seemed pretty against having people in his house, didn't he? He seems to have some mental health issues around cleanliness – could it be OCD? And the church houses are rented out or used for, um, other stuff. I guess maybe they needed a central hub. Somewhere that belongs to them all rather than each individual leader or congregation. It's certainly big enough to hold a large group of people if we were to get rid of this weird set-up of chairs."

"But why pick *this* place?" Annie asked. "Right out in the middle of nowhere, we're miles from any of the church houses. The nearest one is near Orla Finch's home, isn't it? If I've got my bearings correct."

"Yeah," Swift said. "It's a couple of miles that way."

He pointed in the direction they'd arrived from.

"Oh," Annie said, surprised. "Just a couple of miles. I thought we were further inland. Anyway, why here? Why this barn? And why does it look so bloody awful from the outside?"

"All good questions, O'Malley," Swift said, as he made his way to a small door at the back of the barn. "Are you sure you made the right decision when you left the force?"

"Hey," she said, whacking his shoulder. "I just tried to look into a covered-up window with a phone torch."

"Swings and roundabouts," he laughed, trying the handle of the door.

Annie stood back a little as the door swung open towards them. "Swings and roundabouts," she whispered, almost to herself.

"Know what my guess is?" Swift said, feeling around on the wall inside the next room for the light switch. "They don't want anyone looking in on them. They want to keep this a secret. And what better way to hide a secret, than in plain sight?"

Annie heard the click as he found the switch, followed by Swift's sharp intake of breath. "Holy Mary Mother of…" His voice petered out and Annie caught a glimpse through the door as he walked into the room.

The room was small but made to feel much smaller by the fact that absolutely everything was painted womb red. The floor, the ceiling, the walls. She took a tentative step inside, pushing the door as wide as it would go with her foot. There was no way she wanted to get trapped in this place. There was one small blackened window and no other way out. At the far end of the room was an altar. At least, Annie thought it was an altar; four foot deep, it took up the length of the wall and was covered in lacquer that made the red paint look like a pool of blood. At each corner was a squat candle, half-burned. And right in the centre of the altar, glistening with the reflection of Annie's phone torch, was a small sickle, as clean as the day it had been bought.

'What the hell?" Annie said, taking a step towards it.

Swift shot his arm out and stopped her, mid-step.

"Don't touch it," he whispered, and the drop in his volume made Annie want to flee the whole building.

"What?" she hissed back.

"Don't touch anything else," he said, still quietly, as he tiptoed carefully up to the makeshift altar. "There may be forensics here. This whole place looks like it may be swimming in forensics."

"You mean—" Annie started, not wanting to put into words what was going through her head. "You think that's actually blood?"

Swift grimaced. "I don't know. Maybe. I want to go and poke it with something. Have you got a pen on you?"

Annie nodded but immediately regretted it. She had her favourite pen, the one she chewed without even thinking about it. She dug into her pocket and reluctantly handed the pen to Swift.

"Can you poke with the writing end?" she asked, thinking how little she wanted to throw it away. Of course, she'd have to if it came back dripping with the blood of an unknown and probably unwilling donor.

Swift raised an eyebrow, but to his credit he flipped the pen around and approached the altar with the lidded nib first. She heard the tap as the pen hit the surface. Nothing moved, the slick red top of the altar didn't dimple or ripple. Swift dropped his hand and sighed.

"Oh, thank God," he said, handing Annie her pen back. "It's not blood. It's just very well polished. Jeez, I thought this was going to be the site of some sort of bloody ritual."

"It still looks like it might be," Annie said. "Never mind that there's no blood here now, it looks like the Angels are preparing for something weird. When is their ten-year anniversary party?"

"Saturday," Swift said, turning back to Annie, and searching her face. "Tomorrow, or today depending on what the time is right now."

"So, what do we do?" Annie asked.

"We can't tell them we broke in," Swift said. "If there's any evidence here of the missing girls it'll be inadmissible in court. I think we need to stake this place out and watch what happens tomorrow."

"Me too," Annie agreed. "There are too many links here to ignore. The markings on the walls, the altar and sickle…the fact it's in the middle of a bloody great big cornfield and whoever took the girls left a doll shaped out of the stuff. Can we tell if the dolls are made from the same corn that's in this field?"

"We can certainly try," Swift said.

"What if they're going to sacrifice those girls?" Annie blurted, keen to get the words out of her head. "Sacrificial virgins, or something." She shuddered.

"If they're going to do anything like that with Orla and Jodie then at least we know they're still alive right now and will probably be kept alive until they're needed,"

Swift said, scratching his stubble. "But that seems a bit far-fetched, don't you think?"

"Well, maybe," she replied, feeling a bit daft. "But just look at this place. What else do you think is going on here?"

"I have no idea, O'Malley," Swift said. "No idea at all."

NINETEEN

M<small>AGGIE</small> F<small>INCH'S</small> <small>HOUSE LIT THE WAY ALONG THE COASTAL</small> path like a lighthouse as Annie and Swift pulled up outside the door. It was nearly midnight and Annie didn't want to wake the heavily pregnant woman this late, but judging by the glare leaking out from behind the curtains, it seemed that she wasn't asleep. They'd taken the coastal road home from the barn, only after Swift had jimmied the broken door back onto its large metal hinge. From a distance there was no evidence the door had been tampered with, and Swift had questioned as he pushed a slat back into place, if they'd even report the damage to the police.

"Is there news?" Maggie asked, pulling the door open, her face gaunt and drawn in contrast to her swollen belly. "Has something happened?"

Swift shook his head and quickly put a stop to whatever horrors were going through Maggie's mind about their late-night visit.

"We were in the area and wondered if we could ask you a few more questions, Miss Finch?" he said, smiling at the harassed woman.

"Of course," she said, opening the door and welcoming them in. "Anything I can do to help."

"Sorry if we woke you, Maggie," Annie said, squeezing her arm gently as she passed.

"Not at all," Maggie smiled, rubbing her bump. "What with the pain of missing Orla and the Braxton Hicks of this one, I'm not sleeping all that much. Especially at night. I can't stop thinking about Orla, all alone in the dark and calling for me."

Silent tears tracked down her cheeks. Annie took her by the elbow and led her through to the small living room they'd congregated in the last time they had been there. As Maggie took to a dining chair, Annie remembered the advocate who had been there before, silently making herself known with tea and biscuits and the quiet kind of support that Maggie could do with right now. The psychologist in Annie was bursting to do the same, so she gave Swift a look, pointedly directing her eyes towards the kitchen. Swift agreed. Annie could kill for a soothing cuppa herself after being in that unsettling barn, but before that could happen, she still had the pressing matter of her bladder to deal with.

She made her way down the dark corridor to the kitchen, listening to Swift talk to Maggie about the Angels of the Water. She filled the kettle and flicked it on before tiptoeing to the back of the house and the bathroom. Annie hated using public toilets and this was even worse. She could never help but imagine all the germs left there from the previous occupants. To her surprise, the bathroom was immaculate. Obviously the one room in the whole cottage that had been bad enough for the landlord to have to renovate. Sitting down, Annie cast her eye over the reading material—the plastic children's books that they take in the bath and chew, and women's magazines, but the good ones, not the weekly rubbish. Annie pictured Maggie sitting on the lid of the loo reading *Home and Country* as Orla splashed about in the bath, and her throat filled with sadness. Swallowing it down, Annie got up and flushed, a leaflet catching her eye on the reading pile as she turned and washed her hands.

Shaking her hands dry—using other people's towels was a no-go no matter how tidy the bathroom—Annie picked it up. It was another religious leaflet, this time from a real church, a depiction of the cross on the front. It spoke of coffee mornings and cake sales. At the top the advocate, Aila, had written in her own hand how much she'd love to see Maggie there. Annie shook her head; a professional shouldn't be forcing their religious views onto their clients, no matter how well-meaning they were. Still, it was better than joining the Angels, wasn't it?

The staleness of the water in the teapot made Annie think it hadn't been used since their last visit. She wondered if Maggie had had any other visitors during the week. She put the cups and some milk on the tray, sniffing it first to make sure it was okay, and filled a fresh pot with hot water.

"And do you recognise this man?" Swift was asking as Annie returned to the living room with the tray. She'd found a pack of unopened biscuits on the side and her stomach had rumbled loud enough for her to add them to the tray. "His name is Grey Donovan."

Maggie leaned over the table and snatched the picture out of Swift's fingers. "This is the guy?"

Swift and Annie exchanged a look.

"What can you tell us about him, Maggie?" Annie

146

asked, placing the tray down between Swift and the woman and pouring everyone a cup of very strong tea.

"No," Maggie looked up from the picture. "What can *you* tell me? This is the man who Tim was living with isn't it? The police at the hospital asked me if I knew him, they told me his name."

She started to shake her head. "I don't know him. I don't. I told them that. Do you think he has something to do with Orla's disappearance? Was Tim in on it?"

"No, Miss Finch," Swift said. "We don't believe Orla's dad had anything to do with her disappearance. I understand you went to see him in the hospital. You would have seen for yourself that there was no way he could have orchestrated anything like that."

"And *this man?*" Maggie spat the words across the table, flapping the photo she'd grabbed from Swift.

"We're still following that line of enquiry," Swift answered. "So, if there's anything you can tell us about him, or about the organisation who owned the house Tim was staying in, or the other little girl who has been taken, then please try to help us. I know you've spoken to the officers already, but if there is anything you have remembered since then, anything at all, no matter how insignificant you think it might be, now's the time to tell us."

Maggie looked ready to crumble. Annie gave Swift the eye and made him get out of his seat, which he did so with a quiet sulk. Annie took up his vacated seat and reached over to Maggie, gently prising the picture out of her hands. She cupped her own hands around the mother's, amazed at how cold they felt.

"Do you know anything about the local area, Maggie?" Annie asked.

"Only that I wish we'd never moved here," Maggie

said, more tears silently making their way down her face. "I wish Tim had never decided this was the place we'd all be safe. I wish I'd not followed him."

"Maggie," Annie said gently. "It's not your fault, you were in love with him. You have a child with him and another on the way. It's not your fault. You can't blame yourself or Tim for trying to better your lives."

She paused for a beat, stroking the back of Maggie's paper-thin hands.

"What I meant by my question was, have you ever explored the local area, been to any of the Angels of the Water meeting houses, perhaps even without knowing about it? There's a place not too far away from here that they use as a meeting room. An old barn. It's in a field in Flynt."

Maggie looked confused and Annie couldn't say she blamed her. Where was she going with this?

"No," Maggie said, shaking her head. "We only really went places we could walk to. I can't drive, you see."

"Right,' Annie said, and she stopped talking. Something was niggling at the back of her brain and she couldn't quite place it.

"This barn," Maggie asked, drawing her hands out from under Annie's. "Is it important?"

"We think it might be," Swift said, still staring out of the window into the dark night. Annie could see his face in the reflection. He looked tired. "Can you tell us if you've heard anything about the ten-year anniversary party of The Angels of the Water?"

"Only the rubbish that keeps getting posted through the door," Maggie said, waving in the general direction of the front door. "They're very persistent. Aila threw them all away last time she was here; she's very religious herself, proper religion though, very devout. I don't need all that nonsense. But I don't remember seeing anything about an anniversary party. *That* I might have been interested in, if there was free booze and I wasn't like this."

She laughed with no humour and pointed to her stomach.

"Oh God," Maggie's face crumpled. "How can I be joking at a time like this? I'm sorry. I'm really tired. Do you mind if I get some sleep now, I'm not sure how much more help I can be?"

Annie stood up, wondering why on earth they'd decided to stop in on Orla's mum and not just driven straight back to the station, or even to their respective beds.

"We'll be in touch, Maggie," Swift said, turning back to look at her. "Thanks for your time."

They left the weary mother and headed back to the car.

"Interesting," Swift said, as Annie put the car in gear and set off home.

"Which bit in particular?" she asked.

"The men of the Angels have gone on about their anniversary as though it's a massive deal, yet there's been no evidence of that anywhere else. No advertising. None of the women have mentioned it. There's nothing except a bunch of men salivating over the fact their little club has reached its tenth year. That's weird."

Annie nodded, turning onto the dual carriageway back to the city.

"There was something else as well, something Maggie said about the Angels. I'm not sure what it is yet, but it'll come to me, hopefully because it feels important. Do you want dropping at yours or at the station?"

Swift shifted in his seat. "Erm, can you drop me at

mine, please? If that's okay? I need to get some sleep and I think we need to call the troops in early tomorrow. They're not going to like that on a weekend!"

"Of course it's okay," Annie said, glancing quickly at her boss. "That's why I asked."

"Right," Swift said, sharply. "Okay then. Thanks."

They sat in silence for a moment before Annie broke the deadlock.

"You'll need to let me know where I'm going, though," she said. "You may think I'm good at mind reading, but I'm not that good!"

"Right, sorry." Swift shifted nervously in his seat and Annie's intrigue was piqued.

He reeled off an address and Annie didn't need to ask twice where it was. She drove on, jaw almost on the floor of the old Golf. As she came off the dual carriageway she didn't turn towards the city, and her home and the station. She took the road leading out of the city that got wider the further out they drove. The driveways grew longer and the houses larger, until Annie could see nothing but their pitched roofs from the road.

"It's just up here, the next turning," Swift said, his mouth tucked into his jumper.

Annie had never seen him looking so embarrassed. She indicated and turned off the quiet road into a driveway lined with trees. An electric gate shut behind her, she hadn't even noticed it open. She figured Swift must have hit the button on his fob a while ago.

"Bloody hell, Joe," Annie said as she rounded a corner of the driveway and caught a glimpse of his house.

It was what she called *sprawling*. Victorian. Replete with the good kind of ivy and three turrets. She pulled up at the front doors and kept the engine turning over.

"See you in the morning then?" Swift said, hopping out the car quicker than Annie had ever seen him move. "Eight sharp. Thanks for the lift."

He slammed the door shut and was up the steps and in the front door before Annie could pick her jaw up and reply.

"Bye then," she whispered, pulling the car around to head back to her distinctly not sprawling office-come-flat and her pull-out bed.

TWENTY

Orla's scream pierced through the quiet room like a blade. She ran, her breath pumping out in tiny bursts as she tried her hardest to hold it in. Her hands reached out to protect herself from hitting the doorway as she scrambled through it and steamed headlong down the narrow corridor. She could see the kitchen ahead. Only a few more steps and then she'd be there. The back door and the garden outside were waiting for her. She knew that was her destination. She needed to get outside. Then she'd be okay.

Her little legs pumped as hard as they could but the floor in the hallway was always polished to perfection and her socks slid around underneath her. She felt her legs go and landed with a hard bump on her hip, her elbow taking a sharp knock too. Orla tried not to scream out. She didn't want to let anyone know she'd hurt herself. She knew what that meant.

Scrambling back to her feet, Orla started running again. Her eyes fixed on her goal, though she really wanted to look behind her, to check she still had time. The fear fizzed her belly and spurred her forwards. A little cry escaped from her mouth and she smacked her hands over her lips to try and hold it in.

As she sped past the dining room, she caught sight of Jodie curled up on one of the chairs, but she wasn't going to stop. Not now. Not when she was so close. When Jodie came, she had screamed and cried out for her mum all the time. Orla had felt scared by all the noise; she wanted Jodie to stop. She had shouted at her, the same way her own mum did, but the other girl just screamed louder. But at least now, Jodie was quiet.

Footsteps thundered behind Orla and she felt her throat tighten. Not far now. Just a little further. The kitchen was in sight now, the door wide open. Past the clean work surfaces and the tall shiny seats where they had to sit to eat breakfast, Orla could see the glass doors to the garden. The footsteps got louder. The garden was calling her; the sky blue through the glass. Orla knew with all her heart that if she could run to the bottom of the garden, she would be so happy that she would dance. She hadn't danced for ages.

As she moved from the hallway to the kitchen, her feet slid on the marble floor. This time she did cry out as she fell down, her head smacking against the cool tiles. The footsteps seemed to be right on top of her now. Orla squealed, ignoring the pounding in her head, and spun around towards the door on her knees, scrabbling at the floor with her fingertips to propel herself along. She was nearly there. So close she could almost smell the warmth coming from the grass and the earth that she loved to dig her fingers into and get them all muddy. The door handle was in reach now. Orla grabbed it and pulled herself to standing, yanking at it to open the door.

But there was something wrong. There was no movement in the handle. It wasn't dropping down like it normally did when she was occasionally allowed outside. It was stuck. She tugged and tugged but it was no use. She heard the footsteps slow behind her and felt the familiar warmth of breath on her neck. The hairs raised up on her arms and made her whole body tickle.

Got you.

She felt strong arms pick her up, and she kicked her legs out to try and break free.

You're IT

Orla screamed, *NO!*

She wriggled free and fell to the floor, laughing so much it hurt her tummy. She didn't want to be IT, she liked being chased, it was fun. She turned sharply and smacked the legs of the person behind her.

You're IT, she screamed, laughing some more.

She looked back to the kitchen door and grabbed the key from the hook on the wall, letting herself out to the garden and the soft grass and play equipment. She spun around and made herself dizzy. It was one of her most favourite things to do. She giggled as she stumbled towards the swings, her head wobbling on her neck. One of the seats was taken by the new girl who had arrived that morning. The new girl hadn't wanted to play with Orla and that made Orla mad. The new girl was still crying, silently, as she swayed back and forth on the plastic swing seat. Orla ignored her and ran back inside; she wanted to play hide-and-seek.

TWENTY-ONE

Saturday.

"PAGE, I WANT YOU TO SPEND THE MORNING WITH AS many of the congregation as possible, the women. I need you to find out if any of them know about the anniversary this evening and if any of them have been invited." Swift was pacing the front of the incident room like a lion trapped in a cage.

He'd gone over the findings from the previous night with the team, all of whom had been chomping at the bit to get forensics on the barn. They couldn't, though. Annie could see the desperation in their eyes as they all came to the same realisation that Swift had last night. What she and Swift had done was illegal and could jeopardise their case if the girls were somehow linked to the barn.

Last night.

What was that all about? Annie wondered if the team knew about Swift's rather gigantic abode. Not that it mattered a jot to the work he did. It just seemed a little inconsistent with the man currently standing at the front of the room, looking like he'd been dragged through a hedge backwards, then forwards again for good measure.

"Are we any further on with finding and questioning Jodie's dad, Lyle was his name, wasn't it, or was it Brad?" Swift directed that question at Page. "Though I don't think her dad is linked, we need to close off as many of these loose ends as possible, it makes getting a warrant for the real perps a bit easier."

Page was about to reply when the phone rang out. Tink, once again, went to pick it up.

"No, Guv," Page said, when the room had quietened. "Though we narrowed it down to Lyle Baxter, he was in Magaluf when the girls were taken. We have photographic and video proof of him downing a luminous fishbowl on the night in question, courtesy of Facebook. He's still there now."

"Right," Swift said, taking a marker pen and crossing right through the picture of Lyle Baxter on the board. "Thought as much. Not about him chugging ridiculously named drinks, just about him not being involved."

"A fishbowl isn't the name of the drink, Guv," Page said, smirking. "It's an actual fishbowl, usually filled to the brim with whatever alcohol the bar staff can find."

"Right," Swift said again, looking bewildered.

"What happened to your misspent youth?" Annie asked, chuckling to herself at the memory of her last fish-bowl attempt, which was a good few years ago now, but still there in the banks of alcohol-related memories.

The incident room quietened to a hush. Annie could hear the ticking of the old clock on the wall and the rising tide of her heartbeat.

What did I say? she mouthed to Page, who grimaced at

her but, before he could respond, Tink flew into the middle of their line of sight and swore loudly.

"There's been another one," she said, slapping a piece of paper down on the desk in front of Swift.

"Annie, with me," Swift said as he ran towards the door of the incident room, car keys in hand.

THREE-YEAR-OLD KATIE GREEN had been snatched from her buggy outside the Londis a few streets over from where she lived. Her mum had popped in for a pint of milk and left the young girl waiting for her in the street. By the time she'd scrabbled around in her purse for the right change, the girl was gone. A small doll twisted together from corn was left in her place. No onlookers, no witnesses.

"I only left her for a minute, two max," Katie's mum wept into the arms of the family liaison officer already at the house. "I needed milk. It's too crowded in the shop to take the buggy in, and she's getting too heavy for me to carry in my state. She was asleep, she was strapped in."

Annie looked around the small flat. Children's toys littered the floor and the sofa, but something far more sinister littered the table in the corner of the room. Bongs, lighters, tobacco, burnt tin foil, and rolled up notes. Katie's mum caught Annie looking and wrinkled her brow.

"Just because I like to smoke, that doesn't make me a bad mum," she said defensively, through her tears.

"No," Annie said, against her better judgement. "I never said that, Miss Green, sorry, I just…" She stopped talking, wary of overstepping the mark.

"It's *Mrs* Green," the woman sniffed.

"Where is your husband, *Mrs* Green?" Swift asked.

"Look, I already told the officers that I spoke to earlier, Derek's at work," Mrs Green spat. "He has nothing to do with this. Why would he snatch his own child and swap her for a bloody doll?"

"Where is the corn doll now, Mrs Green?" Annie asked, eyeing the Londis bag by her feet that looked like it was stowing more than a pint of milk.

"It was sent to forensics," the FLO answered.

"Why don't you go and make some tea?" Annie asked the FLO, nodding at the carrier bag. "There's milk there if you need it."

She got up and picked up the bag, and the unmistakable clink of wine bottles sang out. Mrs Green looked down at her bitten nails but kept quiet.

"Mrs Green," Annie said. "You said just now, *too heavy to pick up in my state.* What did you mean by that?"

"What do you think?" Mrs Green scoffed, sitting up straight and displaying a small but unmistakable baby bump. "Call yourself a detective?!"

Annie caught Swift's eye and they exchanged a look, but before either of them could speak, Mrs Green butted in.

"Look," she said, rubbing her eyes violently with the heels of her hands. "This has nothing to do with me, why are you here judging me for liking a drink and a smoke when you should be out there trying to find my little Katie?"

Mrs Green's tears started again, in earnest this time. Annie's brain was working overtime; she could feel a connection forming in her mind and tried to leave it be to manifest into something whole.

"I've seen it on the news," Mrs Green continued, waving her hands around. "This *person,* whoever it is, takes children. They leave a calling card. That bloody doll. Surely you must have some idea who has taken these kids, who has taken my Katie? It's been nearly a week since that first girl was taken. What have you been doing this whole time?"

Mrs Green was angry. Annie didn't blame her; she knew what it felt like to miss someone so much you felt like your insides would combust. Especially when you knew they were out there somewhere…if only they could be found.

"We've been doing our best," Swift said, getting to his feet. "Do you mind if we look in Katie's room?"

Mrs Green shook her head. "It's just through there, the one with all the stickers on the door."

Annie and Swift left Mrs Green with the FLO, who had arrived back with tea and some cake she must've found. The internal hallway was dark, no natural light sources lit the space, but they found Katie's room pretty quickly as the flat was so small. Her door was so covered in stickers it was impossible to see the Formica under-neath. Annie shut the door behind them.

"She's pregnant and taking drugs?" Annie said in a whisper.

"Oi," Swift said, rounding on Annie. He was so close she could see just how red his eyes were. "No judgement from us, okay? You should know better, you're a psychotherapist!"

Annie winced and took a step back. "You're right. Sorry."

The room gave up no secrets. It was so full of toys and stuffed animals that Annie had no idea where to start.

"This feels different," she said, carefully picking up a

book that made fart noises. "Hasty somehow. Like the abductor was in a hurry."

"Because she was taken from a shop?" Swift asked, peeling on a blue glove and lifting the unmade covers from the bed.

"I don't know, yeah, I suppose so." Annie didn't know what exactly, but something felt off. *More* off, because replacing children with corn dolls was the most *off* thing Annie had ever heard of. "Do you think the fact that Maggie Finch and Mrs Green are both pregnant has something to do with those kids being taken?"

"Maybe," Swift nodded. "Maybe they know each other through antenatal classes or maybe the perp's wife goes there. I'll get it checked out. But it could just be a massive coincidence. Tammy Carter isn't pregnant, is she? Maybe the perp thought the children would be easier to take from a pregnant woman, harder to chase…"

His voice trailed off as his phone started to ring out.

"Swift," he barked into the handset.

Annie left him to it, keen to get out of the stuffy bedroom. She bypassed the living room, where the FLO was comforting Mrs Green, and wandered through to the small kitchen. The block of flats was built in the seventies, so the kitchen was tiny compared to the other rooms. A frosted glass serving hatch showed the muffled movement in the living room, but other than that there was little to see. The surfaces were clear and clean. The oven was spotless. Annie ran the cold tap and held her hands under it, relishing the coolness on her fingers. The temperature was warming up, and Annie felt distracted by the heat at the best of times. And this was most definitely not the best of times. A noticeboard was tacked to the wall beside the window, home-made drawings and letters were pinned in no discerning order. Underneath one particularly bright painting of a caterpillar, Annie saw a familiar logo poking out. She shook the water from her hands and lifted it carefully from the board.

The Angel rose from the water and stretched up to the sky. Annie heard the bedroom door opening and went out to show her find to Swift. His face looked more drawn than it had five minutes ago.

"Everything okay?" she asked.

Swift shook his head. He took the leaflet from Annie's hand and grabbed something out of his bag before heading in to where the two women were sipping their tea.

"Mrs Green," Swift said, holding out the leaflet so she could see it. "What can you tell me about your relationship with The Angels of the Water?"

Mrs Green spluttered her drink.

"I don't have a relationship with them, this just came through the door."

"But you pinned it on your noticeboard for a reason?"

"I wondered if they did coffee mornings," she said, biting her cheek. "It gets a bit lonely around here when Derek's at work, especially with the little one."

More tears fell as she rubbed her tummy with her free hand. Swift looked as though he'd seen enough. He shook his head and swapped the Angels' flyer for the picture of Grey Donovan.

"And what can you tell me about this man?" he asked.

Mrs Green's eyes narrowed, and her face turned puce.

"No idea who he is." She put her cup down on the table and got out of her seat. "Now if you could get out there and try to find my daughter, I'd appreciate it."

"SIT DOWN, Mrs Green," Swift barked, making Annie jump and Mrs Green retreat to her seat quicker than a greyhound out of the blocks. "It's not about drugs, not right now. I need you to tell me if you *know* him or not. Tell me how, tell me why, tell me his bloody inside leg measurement if you have to, just talk to me."

Mrs Green shrunk into herself. She looked younger than her years, though they were only late twenties from what Annie could gather.

"He sometimes brings me stuff, you know," she said in an almost whisper.

Swift nodded. "And he'd met Katie?"

Mrs Green nodded back.

"Right, well we have just been given CCTV footage outcome, and it looks like Grey Donovan was outside the Londis when you went in for your wine. He's the one who has taken Katie."

TWENTY-TWO

THE 4x4 FLEW ACROSS THE CITY. ANNIE HELD ON FOR dear life as Swift took the corners with some added kerb.

"Did the CCTV guys manage to track Donovan? Find out where he took Katie?" Annie managed to get the words out before yelping again.

"They're going to let me know," Swift said, barely breaking a sweat. "They said he looked brazen. Just walked up to her, unclipped her buckle, and walked away with her in his arms like she was his. Not that there was anyone else around to stop him, mind. But still. They even got him leaving the corn doll, which was—"

The car phone interrupted him.

"Swift!" he yelled, answering the call with a button on his steering wheel.

"Guv?" It was Tink. "I'm sending you the last known whereabouts of Donovan. The CCTV only went as far as the bus station, but he was seen getting on the number 8 which, interestingly, goes right out to the North Norfolk Coast, past both the village nearest to the barn you found, and Amadeus's house."

163

"Get a constable out to both places now. See if we can pick him up en route to wherever it is he's going." Swift hit the indicator and swerved the car around in an arc, ignoring the horns from passing motorists who didn't have a death wish. Unlike Annie's driver, who she figured was fifty-fifty whether or not he cared to make it out of the vehicle alive.

"Also, Guv," Tink continued. "Forensics are back."

"Hit me!" he yelled, honking the horn at an old lady trying to cross the road.

Annie held up her hand as an apology to the woman, who had dragged her shopping cart out of their way, but they were moving too fast for Annie to see if the gesture had been accepted.

Don't unmarked cars have lights you can stick on the roof? she thought, as Swift took them out onto the bypass, which was thankfully lacking in sharp turns and little old ladies. She relaxed a little and listened to the information Tink was relaying.

"The corn the dolls are twisted from?" Tink began. "Forensics found traces of soil found in Norfolk. It's a certain type of clay found only in the county. There's no way to narrow it down to a specific field though, apparently."

"Shit," Swift said, hitting the wheel. "Still, it's a start."

"The baggies we picked up at Donovan's house had no traces of any of the missing girls."

"Double shit!" Swift shouted. "Any good news?"

"Tim Barclay's clothes had traces of his own daughter on them but nothing of Jodie Carter," Tink said, apologetically.

"Fuck!" Swift shouted again. "I asked for good news." He hung up on Tink just as she was saying goodbye.

"We *know* Grey's involved," Annie said, trying to placate him so he'd remove his foot from the accelerator slightly. "We've literally got him on camera taking Katie."

"But where is he taking her and why is there nothing else on him? Surely forensics would have picked up something of Orla on the bags of drugs? Or on Tim Barclay?"

"Where are we going, Swift?" Annie asked, as Swift hit the indictor again and sped off down a slip road.

"We're going back to Jodie Carter's house. I need to get a connection between Donovan and Jodie. Do me a favour and call Tink back. Get her to sort out a proper forensic sweep on Donovan's house now we've caught him in the bloody act. That definitely reaches bloody threshold."

"On it," Annie said, grabbing her phone before it went flying off her knee.

TAMMY CARTER HAD AGED ALMOST fifty years in the few days that had passed since Annie was last at the house. The smell of plug-in was stronger now, and Annie could see why—every plug socket was full. The FLO looked green about the gills and took the opportunity to escape for some fresh air when Swift and Annie arrived. Tammy Carter puffed away on a cigarette and her cheekbones looked like they were going to burst out of her skin. She was a shell. In all of the women who'd had their children snatched, Annie could see her own mum reflected in Tammy the most. It was as though her soul had been sucked from her body, like the victim of a Dementor. Annie's mum had been the same when Mim had been taken away by their dad. Like she needed the love of her missing daughter to fill her shell back up again. That had never happened

165

though, and Annie had a pang of guilt at the length of time that had passed since she'd last spoken to her mum. She made a mental note to call her later, no matter what.

Swift had got straight in there, telling Tammy that there was no news about Jodie, but that they were on the brink of an arrest. Annie hated the hope she saw in the woman's eyes when the police arrived, which was quickly replaced with fear when she realised the police weren't smiling.

"We need you to do something for us, Miss Carter," Swift said, reaching into his bag. He held out the picture of Grey Donovan. "Can you tell us if you know this man?"

Miss Carter's face gave her away as much as Katie's mum's had.

"Is it him?" Tammy nodded at the photo, handing it back to Swift. "Is that who you think has my Jodie?"

Swift nodded but it seemed Tammy Carter had other thoughts.

"What on earth would a little scrote like Grey want with my daughter, and that other girl?" Her face sagged in on itself. "You don't think he's, you know, a *nonce* do you? He never gave that impression when he was here on the estate. He'd always try and get it on with me, not little Jodie. He was a gentleman too, despite the drugs. I quite fancied him. Was he only trying it on with me to get to my little girl?"

With each question, Tammy became more animated. Her arms flew about so much that her cigarette ash scattered all over the sofa. She noticed, and brushed at it frantically with her free hand.

"Shit, shit," she said, before scurrying out of the room and back again with a wet cloth.

"Tammy," Annie said, taking the cloth from Tammy's

freezing cold hand and sitting her gently back down on the damp sofa. "Please, try to breathe. We don't know Grey Donovan's involvement yet, only that he is involved somehow. I know it's hard, but please try not to think of all the different scenarios that could have happened. It'll make you go insane, trust me, I've been there. Jodie needs you to be here and to be strong for her when she gets back, and we need you to remain focused on what we're here to do. What can you tell us about Donovan? Also, when was the last time you ate something proper, or had a hot meal?"

At that, Tammy turned green right in front of Annie's eyes. Annie shifted ever so slightly away from the woman in case she was about to be showered in vomit.

"Please don't talk about food,' Tammy said, swallowing hard. "It's bad enough with the dread that's sitting in my stomach now because of Jodie let alone the morning sickness."

"What?" Swift was over at the sofa in a nanosecond. "Morning sickness?"

"Yeah," Tammy said. "Coming up to sixteen weeks. I remember with Jodie it passed at twelve weeks, so I bet it's a bloody boy."

Tammy rubbed her stomach. Annie caught Swift's eye and he almost imperceptibly motioned towards the door.

"Well, I think we could all use a hot drink. I'm going to put the kettle on," Annie said, getting up. "Swift, some assistance please."

They left Tammy with her FLO, who reluctantly returned inside.

"All three of them...pregnant," Annie said, shaking her head.

"And they all know Donovan—either they've bought drugs from him or have links to someone close who has—

and they're all pregnant." Swift flicked the kettle on so they could talk above a whisper. "Donovan was known to the church; he rents their property. They're all linked somehow to this cult. And I bet it's all going to go down tonight at this anniversary. It's too weird that none of the female congregation were invited, just the men who lead. We definitely need to get eyes on the barn. Watch it unfold, whatever *it* might be."

"DI Swift?" The FLO shouted through from the living room. "I think you need to get back in here."

Annie followed Swift as he weaved past her and through to where Tammy was now pacing up and down the room like a caged dog. They watched as she darted back and forth between the small coffee table and the dresser, pulling open the drawers and throwing pieces of paper behind her.

"Tammy?" Annie made a move towards the frantic woman.

"No!" Tammy cried. "Leave me be, I know it's here somewhere. I kept it just in case."

"Kept what, Tammy?" Annie backed away as Tammy's elbow narrowly missed her nose. It wasn't deliberate, the woman had moved to the hallway and was now searching a stack of drawers.

"This!" she hissed, holding a scrap of paper in front of Annie, too close for Annie's eyes to focus on what was written on it. "This! Take it. Take it!"

She shoved it into Annie's hand and almost ran back to her pack of cigarettes laying on the sofa. With the first drag, Tammy bent over double and started crying inconsolably. The FLO gently coaxed her to sit.

Annie turned the paper over in her hands. On it was

written the name of a road Annie recognised in the less desirable city centre streets.

"What is this, Tammy?" she asked, handing the paper to Swift, who started to scrutinise it too. "What's the significance of that road?"

"It's where that little shit lives," Tammy sobbed, and Annie saw Swift take out his phone. "I went there. It's the flat above the hairdressers, that's his. It was just the once I was there, he really had me fooled. I thought he liked me, I really thought he liked me. But once we'd, you know…he practically ignored me. He'd only come here to drop drugs off for the rest of the junkies on the estate. But I kept that, for some reason. I thought I'd forgotten him. I *tried* to. He might even be this little one's father."

She rubbed her flat stomach, her face green.

"Right," Swift said, making for the front door. "Thanks for this, Miss Carter, this is a great help."

Annie went to say goodbye to the distraught mother; her therapist's instincts to heal were too strong to ignore.

"O'Malley!" Swift shouted, stopping her in her tracks. "Now!"

She gave a little half-wave instead, and then felt like an idiot as she ran out the door behind him.

TWENTY-THREE

"STAY BEHIND ME," SWIFT HISSED AT ANNIE.

They'd arrived at the flat before the backup had, and Swift didn't want to wait for them. Annie thought he had a point, but hadn't Donovan been seen getting on a bus to the coast with Katie? Not bringing her home.

"How long since Katie was taken?" Annie whispered, as they took the metal staircase at the side of the flat as quietly as they could. They'd checked the front and the back of the flat and the staircase looked like the only exit. It broke about a million fire regulations, but at least Donovan could only have one escape route and that was now blocked by Swift and Annie.

"About four hours," Swift whispered back.

Annie's stomach dropped. That was long enough to get out to the coast, do whatever he needed to with the girl, and make it back here, wasn't it?

"So they could both be back here now?" she whispered.

"All of them could be here, that's why we're going in."

"But why take her out to the coast if he's just going to bring her back?" she asked.

"I dunno, get her an ice-cream and build a sandcastle? Have a jolly?" Swift replied, and something dislodged in Annie's brain, dropping slowly like a marble at the beginning of a marble run. She still couldn't quite put her finger on what it was.

"Or maybe he needed to get the church's consent, check this new one's okay for whatever they're going to be doing tonight." Swift grimaced.

Maybe, Annie thought.

"Why do you think Donovan rented the church house when he has this place?" she asked, hoping that he'd moved out of this place and wasn't going to be there waiting for them with a baseball bat, or worse.

"Dunno," Swift said, inching towards the top of the stairs. "But I guess it's something to do with drugs. Maybe it's easier to get to people when you're in the middle of the city?"

Yeah, that's what she'd thought too.

"And…" she started, but Swift held up a hand. The heckles rose on her scalp like little fingers scratching her hair.

"O'Malley," he whispered, crouching down and turning around. His head was level with hers now, his blue eyes ringed in black. "This is going to be the world's worst raid if you announce our visit with a million and one questions."

Annie ran her fingers across her lips like a zip, and bit down on them for good measure. She couldn't help the fact that her mouth worked nineteen to the dozen when she was nervous. And this may have been the most nervous she'd ever felt—after all, she'd left the force the first time around before she'd actually done any real policing.

Fuck, she thought as Swift stood upright and bashed at the door in one slick movement.

"Donovan!" he shouted, making Annie jump. "It's the police. Open up!"

There was a moment's silence, then a scuffle behind the closed door. Swift knocked again.

"This is your last chance, Donovan!" he shouted. "I'm going to break down the bloody door."

Annie glanced down at the street below; people were slowing down, rubber necking at the two officers on the stairs. Then the door burst open and a flurry of grey track-suit came flying down the staircase. Annie stood firm, her body rigid, and flung her arms out to stop the man trying to get past her. Bracing for impact, she grabbed the banister with one outstretched hand — at least that way she'd be less likely to fall to the alleyway below. But the impact never came. The man in the tracksuit circled around as though he was spinning a pirouette. His torso came crashing into the metal bannister and he grunted in pain. Annie saw the reason why. Swift had a handful of grey hoodie gripped in his fist, his knuckles white with the exertion.

"Grey Donovan," Swift wheezed, dragging the young man back up the stairs. "You are under arrest for the abduction of Katie Green. You do not have to say anything, but it may harm your defence if you do not mention when questioned, something you later rely on in court. Anything you do say may be given in evidence. Do you understand?"

Donovan squirmed and grunted. He threw his head back and aimed a mouthful of gob in Swift's direction.

Swift dodged and the spit went flying into the open door of the flat, landing with a nauseating thud on the grubby floor. Annie felt the contents of her stomach turn over.

"Fuck you, pig," Donovan grunted.

Swift's fist flew out quicker than the speed of sound and clocked Donovan's chin.

"Whoops," Swift said, shaking his hand out.

Annie watched as the young man staggered backwards, precariously dangling from the top step. She took a step sideways, there was no way she was going to block his fall now. For a moment, Donovan teetered on the brink of fresh air, his safety on a knife edge.

"Oh for God's sake,' Swift sighed, and grabbed out for the tracksuit again, dragging Donovan towards him.

Annie heard the welcome sound of sirens getting closer; she took the stairs two at a time to go and flag down the cavalry. As she hit the alleyway floor, Annie heard another sound of fist hitting face, and cringed as she heard Swift saying, "One for the road."

THEY'D PUT Donovan in the smallest, stuffiest interview room in the station, but it still looked nicer than the flat they'd dragged him from. He looked a world away from the smart young man that Peter Johnson had talked about. His namesake-coloured tracksuit had dubious stains littered down the front, and his hair could have fried up their chip supper. A sodden red piece of paper towel was clutched tightly in his hand, stemming the flow of blood from a nose that could very well be broken.

"You," Swift said to Annie, as the team gathered around the table in the incident room. "With me. We're going to go and squeeze that little turd for information.

Tink, Page, you guys need to organise a search of his premises. Both of them. Get me as much DNA as you can. Let's find these girls before it's too late."

Annie bolted to her feet and chased Swift as he marched out the room and down to Donovan.

"Donovan," he said, banging the door open so hard that the young man flinched in his seat. "You need to talk. And you need to talk *now.*"

Annie took her cue and pressed down the button on the tape recorder as Swift read out who was in the room and the charges brought against the young man. They sat opposite Donovan and watched him squirm.

"Where did you take Katie Green?" Swift asked, leaning forward in his chair, his elbows sharp on the table. "Where is she?"

"Please." Donovan crumpled in on himself. "She's okay. She's okay. I was just trying to help."

"Don't give me that bollocks," Swift said, banging his hands down on the table. "Tell me where she is."

Donovan started crying. His nose dripped with pink-tinged liquid.

"Tell us about the flat, Grey," Annie asked, tucking her hair behind her ears so she could see past it.

She wanted to bombard him with questions. *Why do you have two houses? What's so special about the flat? How can you afford to rent two places when I can barely afford to rent one, and that's not even a proper flat?* But she knew, from professional experience, that silence often brought more answers than questions. And she was right. Grey shifted awkwardly in his seat and chewed away at his bottom lip for all of about two minutes before he started talking.

"The house isn't mine," he said. "It was never mine. I was using it on behalf of…"

His brow creased. "Hey, can I have some kind of immunity here?" he asked.

"Immunity for what?" Annie asked, getting in there quickly, as she could see Swift was about to boil over again. "Is this to do with the other missing girls?"

Donovan shook his head. "No, well at least, I don't think so. It's drug related. I don't want to go inside. I'm too young and I don't even do drugs."

Annie considered the young man. It had been almost an hour since they'd dragged him to the station from his flat, and he wasn't even clamouring for a cigarette. He had no sign of the tight sweaty sheen from withdrawal, or dark rings under his eyes from crack; no lesions associated with meth, or the mouth chewing and nose wiping from snorting coke. In fact, he looked a darn sight more awake and alive than both her and Swift did right at this moment. It was getting late, and Annie could count the number of hours she'd slept this week on her two hands, so it was no surprise. But it was a surprise that Grey Donovan didn't partake in a little drug sampling himself.

"You're selling drugs on behalf of someone else, aren't you?" she said, a picture slowly forming in her mind.

"Why the hell are we talking about drugs, here?" Swift interrupted. "There are three missing girls out there whose lives are at stake."

"I can't talk about the girls," Donovan said. "I just can't. I'll get in trouble."

Annie gave Swift a look and he backed down. She turned her attention back to Donovan.

"Tell me about the house," she asked. "Who were you using it on behalf of?"

"The Angels," Donovan said, and his shoulders seemed to drop about a foot. "The Angels of the Water. The church who owns the house wanted me to stay there."

"Why?" Annie asked, though she had garnered a pretty good picture by now.

"I wasn't even looking for a place to stay," he said, quietly. "I just had to prove I was worthwhile, you know? I needed to show I am useful. And when the offer of this house came up, it seemed perfect. Then the Angels approached me, some weird guy called Amacus or something. He said he'd pay my rent for me if I did him a favour."

"Amadeus," Swift said. "Seems like you're doing a lot of people a favour here, Donovan."

Donovan shrugged. "What can I say? I like to help people."

Annie couldn't tell if he was being facetious or he actually thought that giving people drugs was a way of helping them.

"I didn't know when I moved in that the guy who owned the house was part of the church. He had no idea what I was doing there."

"And what *were* you doing there?" Annie probed.

"I was selling drugs," Donovan said pointedly, as though Annie should have worked it out by now.

"Selling for the church?"

Donovan nodded, his lip back in his mouth. "They recruited me because of my connections."

"They're a front, aren't they?" she asked, almost hearing the ping of Swift's eyebrows as they hit the roof.

Donovan nodded again. "I think so. The church thing, it's not real, is it? It can't be. It's ridiculous. The women

176

are all brainwashed but the church doesn't actually *do* anything at all."

"Except sell drugs," Annie said.

"Yeah. But no churchy stuff. They just recruit people so they can put the money through the books. But the money rarely comes from their recruits." He barked out a laugh. "You've seen them. Can you imagine people like that having a spare ten grand to join a cult?"

"But what about the girls, Grey? Why did you need to take Katie? Have they moved on to trafficking?" Swift asked.

"I was just trying to do the right thing. To stay out of trouble. Just watch the anniversary thing tonight. Go to the barn. You'll see exactly what they're doing."

"What do you mean?"

A knock at the door had all three of them swinging their heads to see who entered. Tink poked her head in.

"Guv," she said. "There's something you need to see."

"Now?" Swift asked.

"Right now," Tink said.

Swift barked into the tape recorder that they were leaving the room and ordered the PC at the door to stay with Donovan.

"What is it?" he said to Tink. "We're on the brink of a confession of sorts."

"Sorry, guys," Tink said. "But you're going to want to see this."

She handed Swift an A4 piece of paper. Annie leaned over his shoulder to read it too. It was full of numbers and digits that she vaguely recognised from DNA101 class.

"What's this?" she asked Tink.

"It's Donovan's DNA results," Tink said, and Annie

could tell she was like a bottle about to fizz over. "Turns out there is no-one called Grey Donovan."

"What?" Swift said, his face creased.

"The man you have in there?" she continued. "His name is Gary Donald."

Annie watched Swift's face as it fell, his skin sagging around his normally square jaw.

"Gary Donald?" he said.

"Who's Gary Donald?" Annie asked, her eyes darting between Tink and Swift.

"That's not possible," Swift whispered, turning to look through the window in the interview room door. "That's insane."

"What's going on?" Annie asked Tink, her mind racing overtime.

"Gary Donald was one of the children taken by Theobald."

"The organ trafficker?"

Tink nodded slowly. "The organ trafficker."

TWENTY-FOUR

Saturday Night.

Aɴɴɪᴇ's ᴄᴀʟᴠᴇs ᴡᴇʀᴇ sᴄʀᴇᴀᴍɪɴɢ, ʙᴜᴛ sʜᴇ ᴄᴏᴜʟᴅɴ'ᴛ move. In fact, no one in her team had moved for the last ten minutes and the tension in the air was palpable. Swift had yet again given her the opt out of the evening's stakeout but she felt like the end was so close she could taste it, but it wasn't going to be the taste she expected. There was no way Annie was missing this part. Though, after nearly two hours of a stakeout in the dark, where nothing had happened except Tink having to escape behind a hedge for a wee, she was almost regretting her decision. Then the leaders had started to arrive. She was now squatting down behind the dusty window at the back of the barn, fearful of moving because the barn was filling up and the corn was noisy.

Swift crouched beside her, his back against the wooden frame. She wasn't one hundred percent sure that what they were doing was by the book; their team was too small to take down the entire church if the girls were brought here. How were the four of them going to get the three girls out? But Annie figured that Swift had a back-up plan. One that she hadn't been able to talk to him about because they'd been in with Grey Donovan all afternoon. Or rather, *Gary Donald* if his DNA was anything to go by.

"You okay?" Swift mouthed at Annie.

She screwed up her face then pointed at her legs, curled under her like pipe cleaners.

"Rookie," Swift mouthed, holding out his hand so Annie could use it as leverage.

She slowly unfurled, the blood rushing back to her feet and cramping the entire length of both legs.

"Ow," she mouthed back to Swift, who was quite obviously biting back a laugh, before his head flicked towards the barn window, his face now serious.

He held a finger up to his lips as the lights in the barn dimmed and started moving. They'd lit the candles. Through the gap in the dusty window, Annie could see a flickering now, as though she was looking through a zoetrope. The men moved in stuttered steps; their arms held skywards like the Angel herself. Annie shuddered, her skin twitching with nerves. There must have been ten leaders in the barn, all of them male, all of them dressed from head to toe in white robes. It was like something out of a movie; one that Annie wouldn't watch because she lived on her own and wasn't a fan of nightmares.

Through the wooden slats she could hear a kind of chanting start up; low, rhythmic, steady. It sent her already jelly legs into a state of catatonic fear.

"What the fuck?" she mouthed to Swift when he removed his gaze from the window.

Weird," he mouthed back.

He touched his earpiece and whispered, "No sign of Amadeus, yet. Keep me updated."

The rest of the team were camped out at the entrance to the track leading to the barn. They had eyes on the road, and they had a warm car to sit in. Not that Annie was cold, far from it, the shivers she had weren't due to the weather.

The chanting grew louder and more forceful. All the doubts Annie had about the leaders sacrificing the missing girls flew right out of the window. If they could stand around inside a derelict barn and chant to goodness knows what deity, then a little bit of bloodletting wasn't going make them bat an eyelid. Swift tapped her shoulder and they moved silently around the side of the building, still under cover of the corn as well as the new moon. They stopped under the window of the side room, the one with the altar and the blood-covered tablet. Swift peered carefully over the sill and ducked quickly back down.

"They've moved into here," he mouthed.

Annie dragged herself to the windowsill and peeked in. The men were all gathered around the altar, a semi-circle of white cloth swaying to and fro. She could see the back of Peter Johnson's head, and a bald patch which she recognised as belonging to Richard Able.

"Jeez," she mouthed, ducking back down and leaning her back against the side of the barn.

"There's something fucked up going on in there right now," Swift said, upgrading to a whisper.

He tapped the side of his head and Annie thought he was indicating how crazy they all were, but as his eyes widened, she realised he was listening to the team in his ear.

"He's here," he hissed at Annie. "Amadeus has just

pulled onto the track. The windows of his car are blacked out, but Tink said there's definitely someone in the back."

This was it. Annie's whole body fizzed with nerves. She heard the crunching of tyres over the gritty track and the ticking over of the engine as Amadeus pulled to a stop. Annie and Swift stared at each other, their eyes not wavering as she counted not one, not two, but three car doors open and close. Amadeus almost had a car full. With three girls in the back that would make sense. Swift breathed into his hand as he whispered something to the team.

"Stay close," he whispered to Annie, unwarranted, as there was no way she was leaving his side now.

Both of them lifted their heads up to peer into the window. Annie could kneel on the scratchy floor of the field and be at a perfect height. Swift crouched slightly so the top of his head wasn't so prominent. Luckily there was no light behind them, and the window was dirty enough to cover their faces from the inside. But, as Annie watched the men swaying more violently now, she didn't think they'd even notice her if she knocked on the glass and read them their rights anyway. They seemed to be in a sort of trance. Hypnotised by the chants and the candlelight and the smell of some sort of joss stick that was wafting out into the night.

She watched as Amadeus entered the room. His body lit up like a deity himself as he passed through the door between the well-lit large room and the sacrificial room. Dressed in a slick black suit, he was mafia-esque, the complete opposite to the white-robed leaders. Annie held her breath as the chanting silenced; all eyes turned to Amadeus as he raised his hands in a salute.

"Angels of the Waters," Amadeus's voice boomed out through the walls of the barn. "Welcome."

A loud cheer rang through the group of men. Annie could see movement in the barn behind Amadeus but she couldn't quite see who was there, it was just shadows.

"This is a special night for us," Amadeus continued, not moving from the doorway. "A celebration of our birth. A remembrance of the night the Angel rose from the waters of the Broads and greeted us like family. We celebrate not only the original Angels, but all the new Angels who have joined our congregation since."

Another cheer rang out. Amadeus's face twisted into a grin that turned Annie's stomach.

"And as such," Amadeus continued. "I have a very special treat for you all tonight."

No cheer this time, just a silence that swept over the crowd. Amadeus stepped back.

This was it. The moment Annie and Swift had been waiting for. The moment that Grey Donovan, or Gary Donald, had told them to be prepared for. Swift grabbed Annie's hand and squeezed it so hard that her knuckles ground together. She was too on edge to notice the pain.

"Leaders of the Angels," Amadeus cried, stepping forward, a hand in each of his as he led two naked women into the fold. "Welcome to your newest recruits."

"What?" Swift barked, forgetting himself for a moment. "Who are they? Where are the kids?"

Annie couldn't speak, she was too busy watching the robed men close in on these two unsuspecting women like coyotes. But as the women broke free of Amadeus's grip they didn't cower like Annie would have done, butt naked in a room full of strangers. They started to dance, gyrating like pole dancers without their poles.

"These aren't new recruits, Swift," Annie said, prodding the DI in the back as he hissed into his earpiece for the team to check the car.

"What?" Swift said, spinning on his haunches.

"They're not new recruits," she repeated. "Look at them. They're quite obviously comfortable enough to dance naked around a bunch of drooling men. I'd bet my life savings—which are pretty non-existent, but even if they weren't—that they're strippers or prostitutes."

"This makes no sense," Swift said, running his hands through his hair. "I was so sure that Amadeus had those kids. Where the hell are they?"

Annie turned back to the window and watched the men losing it over the sight of the women. The chanting had been replaced by some sort of dance music, a tape recorder in the corner of the room belting out a heady bass as one of the women climbed on top of the plinth and started pouring red wine all over herself. The other, obviously spurred on by her friend, dipped her finger in the wine and started drawing a symbol on her impossibly flat stomach. It was the five-pointed star surrounded by a circle, only it looked different. Annie's brain whirred.

Why is it different? Is it just because it's dripping off the skin of a dancer?

She scanned the room, her eyes darting past the white robes that were quickly being disbanded.

"Swift," she whispered, frantically. "It's Amadeus. He's not in there anymore."

"What?" Swift's head popped up to join hers, his breath hot on the side of her face. "Where's he gone?"

Swift ducked down and crunched his way around the building to the window of the main room. Annie followed close behind. The adrenaline was slowly seeping out of her body now, and she was starting to ache all over; the night air pinched around her hands. They both looked through the clean patch they'd made in the glass and saw Amadeus in the main room with another man Annie didn't recognise. As they shook hands, she saw a pile of taped-up bundles at the door, ready to be lifted from the barn.

"Are you seeing that?" she asked Swift.

"Yep." He held his hand to his ear. "Alert the drugs squad, they're going to want to get here ASAP."

"This was never about those girls, that's what Grey was saying," Annie whispered. "This was always going to be about drugs."

"So where the hell are those girls?"

"Shit, Swift?" Annie's brain finally clicked all the pieces that had been annoying her into place. "Satanism. That's it, it's not Satanism, it's Wiccan."

Swift's eyebrows knitted together.

"What?" he said. "What are you on about?"

"The symbols, I've been reading them all wrong!" She smacked her hand onto her forehead. "Swift, I need to see those symbols from Orla's bedroom again, and the ones from Jodie Carter. I think we might have this all wrong."

"Shit," Swift said, as he shifted on his knees and looked at Annie. 'What have I done?"

The sirens broke their gaze, cutting through the quiet night like a foghorn. Annie watched as Amadeus pushed the other man out of the way and hurtled out of the barn. He didn't get far. Swift and Annie raced to the front of the barn just in time to see him thrown to the floor by a uniformed officer.

"Get Tink and Page to Tammy Carter's house and drive me to Katie's!" she shouted to Swift.

TWENTY-FIVE

"SHIT, SHIT, SHIT," ANNIE SAID, TAPPING AWAY AT Google on her phone as the 4x4 raced down the country lanes. "I was focusing too much on the ritualistic meaning of the symbols. My brain automatically flew to the Satanical, weird ideologies."

"You weren't the only one," Swift laughed ironically.

"But I think that's the point," Annie continued. "I think we were led down that path by someone who was very cleverly hiding behind the Angels of the Water."

They pulled up outside the block of flats where Katie Green lived. Swift cut the engine and swivelled in his seat.

"Tell me why we're here before we go in, O'Malley," he said, hitching a leg up underneath him.

"Something hasn't felt right since the first abduction," Annie said, feeling her way with the words, because her brain kept scrambling them when she tried to formulate them silently. "I wasn't sure what it was, but I knew there was something."

"Good old gut instinct," Swift smiled. "You were built to be a copper."

"Maybe," Annie quickly batted away the idea. "It was as though we were being pointed in the direction of the Angels of the Water. A great ruse, as now we know they probably had nothing to do with the girls going missing."

"Yeah," Swift said, biting the inside of his cheek.

"But why? Why were we led down that path?" Annie continued. "It was something Maggie said on the very first visit we made to her that sparked my initial doubts."

"Go on."

"Do you remember when she denied knowing the Angels when we showed her the leaflet?"

Swift nodded.

"But then she agreed with her advocate's views on how they were heathens?" Annie said, wide-eyed.

Swift nodded again.

"I wondered why she thought they were heathens if she'd never really heard of them. She's not religious at all. Why would she be praying for someone's soul?"

Swift creased his forehead. "And that made you suspect her?"

"No! But all of the mothers we've seen have been on the wrong side of neglectful to their daughters, don't you think? Tammy leaves Jodie to fend for herself while she has a lie-in. Mrs Green leaves Katie outside the shop while she's in there buying alcohol. Maggie, well Maggie seems different, she's not neglectful as such, but Orla's dad was, and the house is in a state. Then it was something you said," Annie garbled. "Do you remember?"

"You're going to have to narrow it down a bit, Annie," Swift said, his eyes darting between hers. "I've said a lot of things to you since you joined the team on Monday. God, was it really only Monday?"

"About Grey, Gary, Grey, whatever his name is," she

said, gesticulating wildly. "He took Katie out to the coast, didn't he? And *you* said he probably did it to give her a jolly! Get some ice-cream, have some fun. Except as he's not actually Grey, he's *Gary* — a child who was kidnapped at a young age and probably didn't know fun from that moment on."

Swift gathered up Annie's hands in his and guided them down to her lap.

"Breathe, O'Malley," he said. "I get it, I'm the same when I make a breakthrough, there's no better feeling. Except maybe arresting the perp. But you have to remember to breathe. Especially when I have no idea what you're about to say and the whole case could rest on you being able to get out a coherent sentence!"

Annie took a deep breath, trying not to think about Swift's strong hands gripped around her own sweaty little paws. "I think I know who's got the girls. My brain couldn't put all the pieces together until just then, at the barn. When the naked woman was painting a symbol on her stomach with red wine."

"What?" Swift said. "I must have missed that; I was too busy watching the leaders try to catch the wine falling off the other one with their mouths. What a night!"

Annie raised an eyebrow.

"Right, sorry," Swift added. "Looked awful, really boring."

"Focus, Swift!" Annie said, shaking her head but with a smile on her lips. "The symbol, it was a circle with a five-pointed star enclosed inside."

"Like the one we saw in Orla's bedroom?"

"Right." Annie said. "Only it *wasn't* the symbol we saw in Orla's bedroom."

"You've lost me," Swift said. "I'm pretty sure it was a circle with a star inside."

Annie peeled her hands away from Swift's and looked around the car for a pen and paper. She grabbed a receipt from the glovebox and a pen from the centre console and started to draw. Two circles, as circular as she could get them with nothing to lean on. Inside each circle she drew a five-pointed star. The first one had a point of the star at the top of the circle, in the second, the point faced downwards.

"Look," she said, shoving the receipt in Swift's hand. "This one, where the point is upwards, is the sign of the Wiccan. A positive symbol, a sign of—,"

She grabbed her phone and read from the screen. "A symbol of five elements; spirit, water, earth, fire, and air. It's associated with earth; a grounding stabilising element that can bring peace and comfort."

She looked up at Swift.

"And this?" He pointed at the second picture.

"This one is *inverted*," Annie said, almost shouting, turning again to her phone. "It *can* be a symbol of evil. Some believe that it attracts sinister forces because it over-turns the proper order of things."

She put her phone down and turned once again to Swift, who was studying the pictures, his eyes wide.

"I automatically assumed, because a child had been taken, that we were looking at the inverted pentangle meaning. But," Annie said, hammering her finger down onto the first picture she drew. "But this is the symbol that we saw in Orla's bedroom. The Wiccan symbol of faith. And the triquetra, I thought it meant the three beings; father, son, holy spirit. But if the five-pointed star is pagan, then the triquetra could be intended to symbolise the life-cycle of the woman. And this all makes sense now!"

"To you maybe!" Swift huffed.

"Don't you see?" Annie added, breathless. "The corn doll wasn't a warning, it was a protective talisman, a symbol of fertility. God, I'm so stupid."

"So, what does this mean?" Swift asked, leaning in. "And why are we here?"

MRS GREEN HAD TAKEN on the hollow look of the two other grieving mothers Annie had seen that week. It was a sort of lost look, perhaps worse than grief, as they were stuck in the hellish limbo of not knowing where their child was or if she was safe. Annie knew that people often filled in gaps in information with worse case scenarios, but in this case, maybe they were right to.

"Mrs Green," Annie said, sitting on the edge of the sofa. "When we were last here you touched on the fact that you knew Grey Donovan, that he was your drug dealer, is this right?"

"Have you turned up here at a ridiculous time to accuse me of something?" Mrs Green looked like a cat caught in a trap.

"Quite the opposite," Annie said strongly. "Please just answer my question."

Mrs Green huffed, but her energy soon sapped.

"Yes," she sighed. "That's right."

"And when did you start taking drugs? Buying from Grey? Were you pregnant with Katie?"

Mrs Green shot to her feet and spun to face Annie, her finger right up in Annie's face. Annie held her breath and waited for the onslaught of abuse. But it didn't come. Instead, the mother collapsed onto her haunches, her hands covering her face as she sobbed. Annie stroked her on the curve of her back.

"Please, Mrs Green," she added. "I'm really not here to judge you. I'm trying to piece together something, and this information would be really helpful."

Mrs Green sniffed and dragged her dead weight of a body on to the seat next to Annie.

"I *was* doing drugs when I was pregnant with Katie," Mrs Green said, wiping her nose with her sleeve. "But I only met Grey a few weeks into *this* pregnancy. He was too hard to say no to, you know? I thought he liked me, and I was lonely with Derek being away at work all the time. Looking after a little one is hard work on your own."

"So he seduced you?" Annie asked.

"Kind of, I guess so, yes." Swift handed Mrs Green a tissue and she took a moment to compose herself. "I met him down the local. I'd not seen him before and he's a good-looking guy, you know? I think he cottoned on to the fact I was lonely."

Annie nodded, her thoughts coming together. "But back when you were pregnant with Katie, you were taking drugs, just not drugs from Grey?"

Mrs Green nodded.

"Did you ever have any contact with Social Services?"

Mrs Green's eyes narrowed. "Why?"

"Please, Mrs Green, just answer the question." Swift spoke now.

"They came to visit me," she said, her face screwed up with the memory. "They said I wasn't a fit mother because I was smoking crack. They wanted to put me on a tiered programme to make sure I was able to look after my unborn child."

"And what did that programme entail?" Annie asked, edging forwards.

"I dunno," Mrs Green shrugged. "I never had to do it in the end, I was given the help of a worker who got them off my backs. She did also get me off the crack. A godsend, really."

"What was her name? This worker?"

Mrs Green screwed up her nose and stared out into the distance. Annie saw Swift about to speak and held up a hand to stop him.

"Alma," Mrs Green said, eventually, her face lighting up. "Aileen, something like that."

"Aila Clough?"

"Yes, that's her." Mrs Green's face dropped. "Why?"

Annie stood up and took Mrs Green's hand. "Thank you. You've been really helpful."

As they were heading out to the car, Swift's phone shrilled out of his pocket.

"Swift," he said, beeping the car open so Annie could get inside.

Swift was right, there was no better feeling than this. The threads of thought that had been floating around for the last week were finally knotting together and Annie had woven an almost complete picture. She climbed into the car and got out her own phone. Guessing that Swift was talking to Tink, Annie dialled the office number and wasn't surprised when Page answered.

"You're back in the office already then?" she said, buckling herself in.

"Yeah," Page said. "The drugs squad arrived and hauled them all away, and Tink and I were pretty quick at Tammy's place."

"Great!" Annie said. "Did you get hold of the info?"

Annie heard the shuffling of paper.

"Yeah," Page said, clearing his throat. "Tammy Carter was under the eye of the local authority when she was pregnant with Jodie, something to do with the people she was hanging around with. They didn't take it too far, you know, just gave her some support to remove herself from that crowd."

"Yes!" Annie cried. "I knew it."

"But get this," Page continued.

"Don't tell me," Annie interrupted. "Aila?"

"Yeah," Page said, the surprise evident in his voice. "Is this your doing?"

Annie made a noise that could have been a confirmation.

"Well done, Annie," he said, as Swift slammed the door and started the engine.

"We haven't found them yet," she replied. "Do me a favour though, would you? Can you contact the Social Services Emergency Duty Team and get them to look up Aila Clough's details? I want an address and phone contact, and a list of any other potential targets that she's worked with. Mothers who she's helped, who are now expecting another child. We're on our way back to the station now."

She reeled off the Social Services number and hung up. Swift laughed.

"What?" she asked him.

"Who died and made you the new DI?" he said, pulling out into the road and flooring the 4x4 back to the station.

TWENTY-SIX

"We know who has the girls, Grey," Annie said, her voice less compassionate that it had been the last time she saw the young man. "So we need you to tell us why you took Katie and where. Or we'll be adding obstruction of justice to a rap sheet that's already long enough to send you away and throw away the key. You've got an hour."

Grey Donovan's eyes were staring right at her. Or through her, Annie couldn't quite tell. It was Sunday morning, so maybe he was just as bone tired and living on adrenaline as she was. She'd downed a cup of coffee when they'd got back to the station and her brain was like Crazy Frog in a blender.

She slammed the cell door shut and trudged back to the incident room.

"I've told him we know who has the girls," Annie said, not waiting to see if she was interrupting. "So let's see if he coughs up Aila's address quicker than Social Services do, because there is nothing recorded anywhere for an Aila Clough."

Page was still on the phone, the hold music loud

enough to hear on the other side of the office. It grated, but Annie thought that most things were grating now she was a week deep with no sleep. Eventually, after a short conversation, Page slammed the phone down and ran his hands through his hair.

"No go," he said, wincing.

"What's a no go?" Annie asked, perching on the table. "They won't give out information?"

"No. Aila Clough hasn't been an employee of the council for about eighteen months. Turns out she was let go because she had downloaded some confidential information and taken it out of the building."

"Let me guess?" Annie said, hopping back down and walking over to the covered noticeboard. 'Names and addresses of vulnerable children in the county."

"Pretty much, yep," Page nodded.

"Could they give a last known address?"

Page shook his head. "No. Advocates aren't directly hired by the council, they're outsourced. So, although she had access to their files, they kept no records of her. And the advocate service has been disbanded due to cuts to the system. So, I can't even get hold of them to ask for her address."

"That's it!" Annie cried. "I knew I recognised her, Aila was protesting outside the station when I first arrived. She was protesting cuts to the service even though she lost her job way before they cut the advocacy. I *knew* I recognised her. What time is it?"

Swift looked at his watch. "A little past eight."

"Right," Annie said, addressing the room. "We need to get out there and find her. Rose said the protestors are there every day, weekends included. Swift, with me, we can stake out the front of the station. Page and Tink, get onto the electoral register, or the gas board, anything, there has to be a record of her somewhere."

The three officers stood to attention.

"I told you," Swift said to Page and Tink, raising an eyebrow.

"Shut up," Annie said, grabbing her coat and heading out to the reception.

Annie spotted Aila through the station window the moment the sliding doors had come to a close. She held her breath and turned away, not wanting to give away what she knew and make the woman flee.

"Swift," Annie said, trying to look casual. "She's there. The one protesting with the banner that says *advocate not antagonist*?"

Swift leant over the unmanned reception desk, picked up the phone and called through a code that Annie didn't recognise.

"Uniform are on their way," he said, putting down the phone and staring at Annie. "They're going to round her up and bring her in the front. That way she can't really do a runner."

Annie felt a pool of trepidation building in her stomach. Then the doors burst open and Aila joined them in reception flanked by three officers, a smile on her face as though she was out for a jolly. Swift stepped up, his sleeves rolled to his elbows, and read Aila her rights as she looked right through him, her eerie smile giving Annie a cold shiver.

"Aila Clough, do you understand why you're here?" Swift asked when they were all safely hidden away in the interview room.

"I want a lawyer," she said, still smiling politely at him and Annie across the table.

"Just tell us where the girls are, Aila," Annie said. "Are they hurt? What have you done to them?"

"Done to them?" Aila said, her dream-like smile still etched on her face. "Hurt them? Are you stupid, girl?"

She started laughing. A long, drawn-out melodic laugh that made Annie's hair crawl. Swift bashed a fist down on the table but Aila seemed to like the drama.

"Oh," she said, grinning, hunching her shoulders up in joy. "We do like to shout, don't we? Do you know what I do when they shout?"

Neither Annie nor Swift spoke.

"Well, I'll tell you anyway," Aila continued. "I give them a hug and a kiss and a bar of chocolate. Because all children shout, don't they?"

She looked up at the corner of the room to the camera and gave a little wave.

'Of course," she added, her cheerful voice almost soporific. "If they keep shouting then I'll wash their mouths out with bleach and shut them in the cupboard, because you do have to have a little discipline too."

"Where are they?" Annie asked again.

With a movement that was slow and assured, Aila turned to face the psychotherapist. "You don't need to know that, dearie. They're safer than they have *ever* been. Even if they're never found, they've had a good few months, or days in some cases, to live the life of a child, rather than the life of a nuisance or a reject. You've only just clocked on to the fact I've been rescuing these children, but it's taken you ten years to get to this point."

Annie's blood ran cold, how many other children had Aila abducted in those years, and where were they?

"Tell us, or we'll throw the book at Grey," Annie said, steeling herself for what she guessed was coming.

"You've got Grey?" she asked, the whites of her eyes bulging, the smile finally dropping from her face. "But… but he's… you need to let him go right now!"

"We have video footage of him abducting Katie Green," Swift said.

"Stupid, stupid boy," Aila scoffed, clapping her hands together over and over. "He thought he was doing me a favour. Thought he was all grown up. He wanted to prove to me that he could do it on his own. But he has no idea."

"Does he know you abducted him as a young boy?" Annie asked.

"I didn't abduct him," Aila shouted, banging her fists on the table and making Annie jump. "I *rescued* him. He was the first, he started it all. He could have been taken by that child molester and had his organs ripped out of him, his parents would never have known. They were a waste of space who were so out of it on drugs that they didn't care when I took him from right under their noses. Literally. I've looked after him like he was my own for fifteen years."

"Did you find the girls through the confidential records you stole from Social Services?" Annie asked.

Aila huffed out air through her nose. "They sacked me for no reason. They didn't need the extra work. All those social workers worked to the bone. They should be thanking me for saving them a job. Like I said, it's not like anyone noticed the girls were missing until now."

"How did you find them? Once your access to records had been stopped?"

"My Grey may not be the world's best son, he has had his troubles, but he has never done drugs." Aila puffed out her chest. "But he knew people who knew people and I still had the old records. I kept an eye on the mothers, stalked their social media, and followed them through the city. I'm clever like that. People often plaster their baby news all over the place. Some of the mothers still wanted my help, and who am I to turn them down? Then it was just a matter of sending Grey in to do the rest."

"He'd get to know them? Supply them with drugs?"

Aila burst out laughing. "It was as though the Angels of the Water wanted to rid themselves of sin by providing me with the ultimate front. I just approached that weirdo Amadeus and offered him Grey's assistance. Added a few red herrings along the way too!"

"The symbols and the corn dolls?" Annie said, her eyebrows furrowed. "But they're symbols for good not evil. Why would they point the finger at what you believe to be an evil cult?"

"You're a little too smart for your own good, young lady." Aila spat the words at Annie. "I couldn't very well mark those poor girls with an *actual* curse, now could I? Thought a few well-placed but mis-guided artifacts might help point the finger at the Angels. Goodness knows they're evil themselves. Bringing that *stuff* into our beautiful county."

"How did you know they were a front for running drugs?" Swift asked.

"Anyone with half a brain could see they were running something, and that certainly wasn't any sort of worship!"

"So Grey would supply the drugs and you'd, what? Swoop in when they were out of it and steal their children?" Annie was incensed.

"If people aren't good enough parents, then who are you to judge someone who is?"

Annie shook her head. There was no reasoning with the woman.

"Who looks after the children when you're here, protesting for a job that you screwed over?" Swift asked.

"They are capable of looking after themselves for a few hours," Aila said, without a thread of irony. "And Grey will pop his head in to make sure they are behaving. There are strict punishments for any girl who misbehaves."

"And Grey took Katie? Why? We need you to tell us where they are."

Aila's nostrils flared. "He is my life, that boy, but he has ruined everything. Ruined it. I guessed you'd be on to me sooner or later, as soon as Katie arrived at my door. But they'll be okay. I made sure of it. I've said my good-byes and they have each other. Soon it will all be over."

"Tell us where they are, Aila!" Swift shouted.

"I won't tell you," she said, quietly. "I won't. I won't. I won't."

With each word the volume increased until Aila was screaming them over and over at Swift and Annie. Bits of spittle flew out of her mouth and hit the table like tiny white raindrops.

"I won't! I won't! I won't!"

Swift grabbed Annie's upper arm and was about to drag her from the room. But Annie pulled away, slamming her hands down flat on the table and staring at the hysterical woman.

"You tell me where you have hidden those girls, right now," she hissed. "Or I will march right into Grey's cell and tell him you're not his real mother, so help me God."

TWENTY-SEVEN

FOR A SPLIT SECOND, ANNIE COULDN'T MOVE. SWIFT WAS counting to three in the background, the uniformed officers primed with the battering ram at the plastic door that wouldn't yield to her hand. She'd tried the letterbox, lifting it with her fingers extended and shouting out to the girls inside, but the only thing she'd been greeted with was a stench that she couldn't clear from her nose.

Swift had smelt it too. He'd paled and stepped aside for the officers, shouting a countdown for any listening ears, trying to stave the fear the girls must be feeling. Annie hoped they were feeling fear, at least that would mean they were still able to feel.

The door cracked open and adrenaline rushed through Annie's body. Heading through the hallway into the house, she called out the names of the three missing children.

"Orla! Katie! Jodie!" she cried, running from room to room.

The house was smack bang in the middle of nowhere, between the church barn and the coast. A sprawling farmhouse, newly renovated and with a security system to match that of Fort Knox. Annie burst through the doors to the kitchen, almost sliding on the newly cleaned floor. The bleach in the air was drowning out the smell of decay that Annie was trying not to think about.

Swift ran into the kitchen behind her and stopped at her back, his hands resting on her shoulders. They both stood still for a moment, their breaths held, listening out for the cries. But the house was silent.

"Oh God, Joe," Annie said, her eyes welling up. "Are we too late?"

It had taken them nearly an hour to get to the house, despite Swift putting his foot down. Annie's gamble that Aila's maternal instinct would be strong enough to protect Grey had worked. But where was Aila's maternal instinct when it came to these girls? Had her own self-preservation won out? She felt Swift squeeze her shoulders and shook the doubt creeping into her head. She had to stay positive.

"You check the garden," she said, turning to face him. "I'll follow the officers up the stairs. This place is huge, they could be anywhere."

"Go," Swift shouted, as he turned the key in the lock and headed out to the garden. "Shout if you need me."

Annie suppressed the need to shout for him right then. She didn't want to be here, but the need to find the girls outweighed her fear of what she might see when she did find them. She headed back to the stairs, near the broken front door, feeling little comfort at the presence of the uniformed officers who stood guard against anyone who might be lurking out in the corn fields. She grabbed the banister rail and dragged herself up the stairs two at a time, all the while shouting for the girls.

Two officers came out of a bedroom, shaking their heads. "Empty, ma'am," one of them said. "And the one over the corridor. Smells like no one has been in them for weeks."

Annie looked. The landing had six doors, the first two ticked off by uniform. The girls had to be in one of the four remaining rooms. There was nowhere else they could be. She steeled herself and pushed open a door, pointing at the room opposite to the officers. The musty, unused-room smell hit her before the door was fully open.

The bedroom was small, a single, with a bed against the middle of the wall and a cross above it. If the girls were in here, then she would be able to see them because it was void of anything else and definitely not lived in. Ducking down and checking under the bed just in case, Annie found cobwebs and little else.

Where were they sleeping if all the bedrooms are unused? she wondered, as she made her way back to the landing.

Two rooms left. Annie's heart was beating its way up to her throat. She heard Swift downstairs, shouting that the garden was all clear. So they had to be here, in one of these rooms. Annie's nose tickled with decay and bleach, and the tears that were threatening to come.

Why hadn't she realised they were being led astray sooner? If she only had, these girls might still have been okay.

"Orla?" she shouted. "It's the police. Katie, Jodie, you're okay now. You're safe. Let us know where you are."

She stopped, holding out her hand to quiet the officers who were coming out of the other bedroom, shaking their heads. The only sounds were the crows in the fields and the ticking of the old grandfather clock in the entrance hallway.

Where are you?

Putting a hand on the doorknob, Annie turned it gently and pushed the door open. Surprised to find herself in a bathroom, an empty one at that, Annie felt her whole body deflate. The taps and floor and bath all gleamed with the cleanliness of someone who had time to scrub at them every day, not someone with three young children running around. In fact, the whole house was devoid of any signs that there were children here at all.

"Clear here too, ma'am," the officer said, sticking his head around the door.

"Where are they?" she said, her nerves so on edge she felt like her jaw would crack.

She shot out of the bathroom and back down the stairs.

"Swift!" she shouted, noticing the DI in the front garden through the broken door. "Can you remember what Aila said about putting the girls in the cupboard when they were naughty?"

"Yeah," he said, making his way back to the house over the neatly cut front lawn. "I was just circling the house, making sure there are no outbuildings. This place is a farm though. There are farm buildings all over the land. But yes, sorry, the cupboard."

"I didn't see any cupboards in the whole house. All the storage was open or hidden by curtains."

"You're right," he said, running his hands over his face.

"Wait a minute," Annie said, her throat closing with emotion. "Didn't you say that Orla was taken when she was playing hide-and-seek?"

Swift nodded. "Yeah, it was her favourite game apparently. She's good at it, but Maggie said that she knew something was wrong when she didn't start giggling when she got nearby."

"I've got an idea," Annie said.

"You think they're still alive?" Swift whispered.

Annie screwed up her face and shrugged. "I can't think of anything else, not until we know for sure one way or another."

"But that smell?"

"Joe," she cried. "Give me this, please!"

"Okay," he shrugged and moved away from the door.

Annie cleared her throat.

"Here I come, ready or not!" She tried to make her voice sound light and fun, but she sounded like the witch from Hansel and Gretel.

A shuffle. Annie and Swift looked at each other.

"Under the stairs?" he whispered, and little fingers of dread crept over Annie's hair.

Annie's heart dropped. She shook her head. Swift raced past her and she turned and ran after him. The stairs were large; the bannisters old, dark wood. The wall where Annie would have expected to see a door was papered over in the same William Morris print that lined the rest of the hallway. Swift felt along the wall, his hands sliding over the paper with a soft scraping sound. She left him to it, instead creeping around the stairs to the kitchen, following the line of the stairs as she went. The top of the stairs sat right above the kitchen, and at the wall that joined the kitchen to the hallway was a pantry door, concealed by a heavy curtain.

"Swift," she tried to speak but her voice came out as a croak.

"You called?" he said, his head appearing at the door.

Annie nodded, not trusting her voice. She lifted a finger and pointed at the grainy wooden door. Swift's eyes widened and then he nodded. Annie lifted the latch as quietly as she could and opened the cupboard door. The smell that escaped made her retch. Her arm flew up and she hid her face in the crook of her elbow. Inside was pitch black, despite the sun raging through the kitchen door.

"Hello?" she said, her voice wobbling. "Who's in here then?"

Silence.

"Come out, come out wherever you are," she added, trying with all her might to stop her fear escaping through her mouth. She didn't want to terrify the girls if they were in here. If they could still hear her.

A long thin tunnel of light from Swift's torch shone over her shoulder and into the dark space. It was red. Blood red. Dark and congealed over the floor and the underside of the stairs. Right at the back, where the stairs met the floor, was an old patchwork blanket that could have once been white. It was hiding something. Something large. Something very still. Too still.

Annie grabbed Swift's torch and moved into the cupboard. It was large enough for her to walk straight into it, though she had to duck as she got nearer to the blanket.

"Annie?" Swift's voice sounded like he was underwater, Annie's blood was pumping so loudly in her ears.

"It's okay," she said, loudly. "You're safe now."

Tears streamed down her cheeks as she spoke. She knew she was too late. The smell. The stillness. They spoke a thousand words even if Annie couldn't. She tiptoed forwards, dropping down to her hands and knees as she approached the blanket. On it, through the dried blood, she could see where someone had lovingly stitched hearts and tiny little daisies. A lot of love had been sewn into the material. With her free hand, Annie grabbed a corner — it was hard and sharp with decay. She pulled it up gently, her breath stuck in her throat.

An arm fell down, knocking her back. She let out a cry. The nails were tiny, just like Mim's used to look when they played dress up as kids. Annie remembered finding them hard to paint because they were like little shells. But these were pale, too pale. Tinged with blue, Annie knew these were not the nails of a young girl who would be able to grow up and paint them a rainbow of colours.

Shuffling back up to her knees, Annie pulled the blanket further up. The arm gave way to a torso, rippled with blue. But as she pulled it higher she heard a noise, a sniff of a small nose. She pulled hard at the blanket and there, amongst bodies that would never see the light again, and bones that had once made up small arms and legs and rib cages, were three pairs of eyes staring up at her, blinking in the torchlight.

"Swift!" she shouted, throwing the blanket behind her as best she could with the weight of it. "Call an ambulance. They're alive!"

She looked at them, each little face illuminated now, pale as the bodies drained of blood, mouths open in fear.

"It's okay, little ones," she said, reaching out for them. "You're safe now. You're safe."

One ran forwards, throwing herself onto Annie, sobbing great wracking tears. Annie stroked her matted hair, hushing her. And as she cradled the small child in her arms she felt something shift inside her, something that had been lodged there since the day her sister was taken. Annie's whole body started to shake with her own wracking sobs.

"You're safe too, Annie," Swift said, crawling in behind her and wrapping his arms around her shoulders.

TWENTY-EIGHT

"How many children had there been?" Annie asked, curling onto one of her therapy chairs and cradling a hot cup of coffee.

Swift sipped his own drink, contemplating the answer; Annie could see it on his face.

"Seven," he said, eventually. "Eight if you include Grey."

Grey Donovan had been reunited with his birth parents the same day Annie and Swift had found the three missing girls. An emotional reunion made harder by the fact Grey was in denial. Annie had been approached by the DCI to provide Grey with some much needed psychotherapy but she'd declined before he'd even finished asking.

"I think I'm too involved with this one, DCI Strickland," she'd said, staring through the window of the relatives' room as two red-eyed adults tried in vain to hug their son. Truth was that Annie had done with listening to other people's problems for a while. She had her own to work through first.

Today was the first day of her compassionate leave.

Her doctor couldn't work out why on earth she would have gone galivanting around with a police team and unearthed a mass grave of missing children if she had been in a sound mind to begin with. Annie didn't have the energy to argue that it had been better for her than the last ten years of her career put together, she was just glad of the time away from the office. So to speak. She was still in her office with Swift now, only it was just her home at the moment, no work was being done.

This? This didn't feel like work.

"Seven?" she said, a flash of blonde hair filling her mind. "So…"

The question was left unsaid. Neither of them needed to say the words.

"Yes," he replied, looking down at the cup. "Four were recovered and their parents found. They were all of an ilk. One that Aila saw herself as better than, because they maybe worked two jobs and had to spend time away from their children. Or they were too drunk or high to notice what their kids were up to."

"God," Annie said. "She's reprehensible."

"Totally," Swift said, nodding, his eyes drifting to the open window.

"What is it?"

"Two of them weren't even reported missing."

Annie's eyes widened. "What? But how did they not get picked up by the social or the police?"

"Aila deleted their records." Swift looked back at Annie. "Over the last ten years she trawled the files of Social Services, took the ones she wanted, then made sure no-one would care. The other two are still listed as mispers."

"Those poor parents."

"Especially given the way she actually treated the children when they were under her care."

They sat in silence for a moment. The birdsong at the window was a welcome loud distraction.

"What happened to them?" Annie asked, eventually.

"The ones who didn't make it?"

"Yes."

"They were what Aila called *bad seeds.* She said they would either learn her ways or they would be punished until they did."

Annie's eyebrows shot up.

"Locked in the cupboard?"

"Not even locked in," Swift said, biting his lip. "God knows what she did to those kids, but they were too scared of her to walk out of an unlocked cupboard to save themselves."

"God." Annie puffed out her breath.

"But the three you saved," Swift said, putting his cup down and leaning over the low table to lift her chin so she had to look at his face. "They're going to be okay. A little malnourished, and they'll need a lot of therapy. But they're alive because of you."

Annie smiled softly. "Not just me!"

Swift sat back in his chair and shook his head. "You were the one who pointed the finger at Aila. I was completely taken by the bloody Angels of the Water. Who have been shut down now, by the way. Amadeus has been arrested for drug trafficking."

Annie laughed.

"Thank God for that," she said. "He's not going to fare well in jail is he? What about the others?"

"They were all oblivious to the drugs. They just joined for the women."

"There's a surprise!" Annie rolled her eyes. "Do you think Grey is going to be okay?"

Swift sighed, getting out of the chair and heading through to the kitchenette. Annie could hear him opening and closing cupboards.

"They're in here already," she called through to him, grabbing a packet of biscuits from the desk. "I keep them near to me at all times at the moment."

She offered him one.

"Thanks," he said, crumbs falling from his lips. "I think Grey is a very long way off okay. Aila took him when he was only five; she pointed the finger at Theobald because it was the same time all that was going on, but really his parents were working all hours to make ends meet, and they used drink as a crutch in a pretty cruel world. They say they never gave up hope, but how do you cope when you think your child has been slaughtered for his organs? Grey's the only one who made it to adulthood."

"I wonder how he did it?" Annie nibbled the edge of the bourbon biscuit.

"I think it was because he was her first," he said. "She didn't want to fail with the first."

"But the more she took, the more unhinged she became?"

"Probably. Anyway, I'd best be off. Top secret police work to be done."

Annie got out of her chair and pulled Swift into a hug. He smelt familiar and safe.

"Thanks for all your help, Joe," she said, pulling away.

"What are you on about?" Swift said, smiling. "I dragged you into it. Thank *you* for your help. If you ever think about coming back to the force, there's always room for you in our squad. CID could use more analytical brains like yours."

"I'm very tempted but we'll see, shall we?" she said, thinking just how much she'd love to join their team, not least to find out more about Swift, his life and his house and the wife who left him, too. "I think I've got a few personal things to sort through first. And my own job to do when I'm ready. Marion really would string you up if you poached me for good."

"Oh God," Swift cried in jest. "I forgot about Marion. She's called me in for a meeting today. I think she's going to throw the book at me for breaking you."

He stopped talking, his face flushed.

"Sorry," he said. "I didn't mean you're broken. I just…"

Annie pushed him by the shoulder, gently, towards the door.

"Best you head off before I break you back then, hey?"

"Bye Annie," he said, resting a hand on the open door.

"Bye Swift."

As the sun set and the night drew in, Annie grabbed her laptop and dragged her weary body into the sleeping bag. She'd pottered about in the flat once Swift had left. Watering her pot plant, dusting, polishing, and hoovering. It gleamed in delight as much as Annie did. With a take-away pizza from Pete, she topped up her wine glass and settled down for a night of *Line of Duty*.

Tapping out her password, Annie saw her emails flash. She clicked, despite the hot pizza and cold wine calling her name. It was this month's bill. She was once again five hundred pounds down the drain and no closer to finding her sister. With a large gulp and a reaction so quick her brain couldn't keep up, Annie whirred off a reply to the private investigator. *Thanks for all your hard work but I think it's time to let this one go.* Signing it off, Annie pressed the send key and let out her breath. Like the moment she held little Katie Green in her arms, Annie felt a lightness she hadn't felt in a long time. Her head floated and it was nothing to do with the wine.

"Cheers, Mim," she said, raising her glass and pressing play on the police drama on screen rather than the police drama in her life.

Halfway through the pizza, just as the tension in the show was ramping up, Annie's phone buzzed on the floor next to her. She picked it up, screwing her face up at the name on the screen.

"Swift?"

"Annie," he replied, and she could hear the sirens in the background. "How do you feel about helping us out again a little sooner than we had imagined?"

THANK YOU!

Thank you so much for reading my book. It's hard for me to put into words how much I appreciate my readers. If you enjoyed Corn Dolls, please remember to leave a review. Reviews are crucial for an author's success and I would greatly appreciate it if you took the time to review Corn Dolls.

You can also find me here:

facebook.com/ktgallowaybooks

twitter.com/ktgallowaybooks

bookbub.com/profile/k-t-galloway

goodreads.com/KTGalloway

Printed in Great Britain
by Amazon

83720737R00130